FORTRESS ENGLAND

Book two in the Secret Squadron series

Recent Titles by Robert Jackson from Severn House

FLAMES OVER FRANCE

FLAMES OVER NORWAY

The Secret Squadron Series

Book One: THE INTRUDERS
Book Two: FORTRESS ENGLAND

FORTRESS ENGLAND

Robert Jackson

The first world edition published in Great Britain 1998 by
SEVERN HOUSE PUBLISHERS LTD of
9–15 High Street, Sutton, Surrey SM1 1DF.
First published in the USA 1998 by
SEVERN HOUSE PUBLISHERS INC., of
595 Madison Avenue, New York, NY 10022.

British Library Cataloguing in Publication Data

Jackson,   Robert,   1941-
          Fortress England. - (The secret squadron)
          1.   Great Britain. Royal Air Force. – Fiction
          2.   World War, 1939-1945 – Aerial operations,   British - Fiction
          3.   War stories
          1.   Title
          823.9'14 [F]

          ISBN 0-7278-5362-7

Typeset by Palimpsest Book Production Ltd.,
Polmont, Stirlingshire, Scotland.
Printed and bound in Great Britain by
MPG Books Ltd, Bodmin, Cornwall.

Chapter One

The Arctic – February 1941

For several hours, a south-westerly gale had lashed the freezing ocean, its strength piling up the waves to a height of thirty feet or more. They rolled up in long roaring swells, dark, foam-flecked, white-crested. The gale ripped sheets of spray from the crests, hurling them horizontally across the water to mingle with icy flurries of snow.

Through the murk and the darkness two great battlecruisers forged steadily on. From time to time a breaker reared up in front of one of them, hung there for a second in a column of ghostly foam, and then collapsed over the forecastle with a deafening roar, shrouding the long bows in a veil of swirling foam before dispersing in gurgling eddies across the anchor chains and through the scuppers.

Four miles separated the two warships. A depth of 1,500 fathoms – 9,000 feet, one and three-quarter miles – of water lay between their keels and the sea bed. This was the Norwegian Deep, the triangle of sea bounded by Norway's North Cape, Jan Mayen Island and Iceland. Some miles to starboard lay the great expanse of the Arctic pack ice, the invisible guardian of the warships' northern flank;

1

ahead was the Denmark Strait, the turbulent waterway between Iceland and Greenland, only 200 miles across at its narrowest.

This was the gate through which the two battlecruisers must crash if they were to reach the North Atlantic.

The mission that lay ahead of them had been meticulously planned and prepared. At various points in the Atlantic the warships would make rendezvous with tankers which would supply them with oil, ammunition and stores. They had already carried out their first replenishment at sea, from the tanker *Adria*, stationed to the east of Jan Mayen.

The warships' mission was to destroy the vital Atlantic convoys that were the lifelines of Britain, a nation that now stood alone against the seemingly all-conquering might of Nazi Germany.

By the summer of 1940, after the collapse of France, these convoys faced a threat from several quarters. Firstly there were the U-boats, covering the North Sea and the Atlantic approaches; then there were the surface raiders, ranging from battleships and heavy cruisers to fast merchantmen converted to the armed raider role; and finally, with the capture by the Germans of air bases on the French Atlantic coast, there was the *Luftwaffe*, whose long-range Focke-Wulf *Kondor* patrol bombers had been wreaking havoc on British shipping for months now. Between August 1940 and February 1941 the *Kondors* had sunk Allied vessels amounting to 363,000 tons, far more than the U-boats or the surface warships.

But the warships were a major threat – there was no

doubt about that. One of them, the *Admiral Graf Spee*, had been effectively dealt with in December 1939, chased into Montevideo harbour by a British naval force and scuttled there on the orders of her captain; but there were others at large, equally as powerful and destructive, if not more so.

Two of them, the battleship *Admiral Scheer* and the heavy cruiser *Admiral Hipper*, had broken out into the Atlantic from their north German ports in the closing weeks of 1940, reaching the open ocean by way of the Denmark Strait between Iceland and Greenland. In November the *Scheer* sank five ships from one homeward-bound convoy, and the toll would undoubtedly have been greater had it not been for the gallant action of one of the convoy escorts, the armed merchant cruiser *Jervis Bay*, whose skipper, Captain Fegen, attacked the battleship and bought just enough time for the rest of the convoy to scatter before his ship was blasted into a blazing wreck and sent to the bottom. Evading strong naval forces sent to track her down, the *Scheer* headed for the South Atlantic, and by the end of the year was operating on the latitude of Cape Town.

Meanwhile, on 24 December, the *Hipper* had made contact with a large troop convoy far to the west of Cape Finisterre, and attacked at first light on Christmas Day. The convoy, however, was strongly escorted, and the German warship was driven off without having caused any damage. She reached the French Atlantic port of Brest two days later and was still there, awaiting the reinforcements that were now ploughing through the Denmark Strait before making another sortie.

The commander of the battlecruiser group, Admiral Lutjens, was grateful for the darkness and the foul weather. The ships had already made one attempt to break through to the Atlantic, but had been frustrated by the presence of British cruisers patrolling to the south of Iceland. This time, with luck and the protection of the weather, they would succeed.

Soon it would be dawn, but dawn in these climes, at this time of the year, meant little. Dawn was a watery greyness on the southern horizon, above which the sun would rise only briefly before sinking from sight again. As the days went by its appearances would become longer, until from May to July it would not set at all. For this was the region of the midnight sun in summer and in winter of the northern lights, those phantom luminous veils that danced and shifted across the polar skies.

With the coming of dawn, the storm abated. The crews of the two battlecruisers increased their alert, but no threat materialised out of the greenish-grey twilight. The hours went by, and at last Admiral Lutjens knew that his battle group was safe. Ahead of the warships now lay the broad expanse of the Atlantic.

Signals flashed between the two battlecruisers, which altered course to the south-west, heading for latitude sixty degrees north. Soon, the long-range *Kondor* reconnaissance aircraft would alert them to the presence of a British convoy, and they would steer to intercept it.

Lutjens knew that his crews were eager for action. They had seen none for eight months, since the end of the Norwegian campaign, when they had sunk the

British aircraft carrier HMS *Glorious* and her two escorting destroyers, the *Ardent* and *Acasta*. Adding to their keenness was the knowledge that they were serving in two of the most powerful warships afloat, each armed with nine 11-inch guns and a formidable array of lesser weapons.

Their names were *Scharnhorst* and *Gneisenau.*

Chapter Two

Atlantic Ocean – 16 March 1941

It was three hours now since the big four-engined Short Sunderland flying boat had lifted away from the waters of Plymouth Sound in the pre-dawn darkness and set course south-westwards into the Atlantic, buffeted by a March wind that was almost a gale, but not quite. Now, several hours later, the aircraft's position was marked by an invisible point on the ocean's surface, designated by the navigator as forty-three degrees north, twenty degrees west. Its intersection of these lines of latitude and longitude placed it some 500 miles west of the outer limits of the Bay of Biscay, and a similar distance north-east of the Azores.

The Sunderland's pilot was a squadron leader and, like the twelve members of his crew, an Australian. In 1939 they, together with the rest of their squadron colleagues, had come to England to take delivery of nine Sunderlands for service with No. 10 Squadron Royal Australian Air Force, but their intention of flying them back to Australia had been thwarted by the outbreak of war. The squadron had been promptly affiliated to RAF Coastal Command

and, based at Mount Batten in Devonshire, had begun Atlantic patrols early in 1940.

The Australian squadron, and others like it – some equipped with Sunderlands, others with American-built Catalina flying boats or with Lockheed Hudson land-based patrol bombers – had soon found themselves locked in a bitter struggle to protect the vital Atlantic convoys that were the lifeblood of beleaguered Britain. On this March day, the Sunderland was due to rendez-vous with a British-bound convoy from Sierra Leone, and shepherd it northwards until it was relieved by another flying boat.

The Sunderland pilot, peering ahead through the wind-screen – the aircraft was running through a rain squall, and the wipers were thumping rapidly from side to side, chasing away the rivulets of water – gave a slight start as a hand tapped him on the shoulder, then looked up, smiled, and reached out to take the enamel mug of coffee that was being offered to him by one of the crew.

The latest air reconnaissance reports, the pilot knew, indicated that the *Hipper* was still holed up in Brest, but you could never be certain; she might have made a break for it within the last twenty-four hours, in which case – if she was heading directly out into the Atlantic – she might be anywhere within the Sunderland's search area.

So might a patrolling *Kondor*, but the squadron leader wasn't worried about that. The Sunderland Mk I was armed with seven machine-guns, four of them in its tail gun turret – two more than the German aircraft carried.

"Navigator to pilot."

The squadron leader put a hand to his face mask, which had been dangling loosely, and placed it over his mouth, flicking the intercom switch as he did so.

"Go ahead, nav."

"We will be in position forty-two north, twenty-one west in fifteen minutes, skipper. Should be sighting the convoy shortly, if it's where it should be."

The pilot grunted over the intercom. "Okay. Can't see much up ahead yet, through this rain. It's looking a bit brighter, though. Just a line squall. We should be out of it soon. Keep your eyes peeled, lookouts."

He glanced at his second pilot, a young United States Navy lieutenant. Officially, Lieutenant (JG) James A. McGill was not there; America was not in the war – not yet, anyway – but the US Navy was cooperating with the British in the war against the U-boat, short of actually sinking the German submarines, and was sending small numbers of personnel to England to fly with RAF Coastal Command in order to gain operational experience. All this was a well-kept secret; if the Germans found out about it, their propaganda people would really go to town. Just in case anything went wrong, McGill had a cover story that turned him into a Canadian.

"Take over for a minute, Jimmy," the pilot instructed. "I'm going back for a pee."

The young American's face brightened at being given the responsibility. He acknowledged the instruction, placed both hands on the control wheel and peered intently into the distance. The Sunderland's captain grinned, undid his harness and clambered out of his seat. Behind the

8

two pilots' seats, the flying boat's flight-deck crew of navigator, radio operator and engineer were all busy at their stations. The captain went past them and along the companionway, past the beam gunners and the mid-upper, heading for the Elsan toilet at the rear of the fuselage. A few minutes later, feeling much relieved, he returned to his place, but allowed the American lieutenant to remain in command for the time being.

It was the keen-eyed co-pilot, in fact, who saw the first sign of the disaster that had overwhelmed the convoy. It looked at first like a dark and threatening cloud, drifting low over the horizon. But as the Sunderland drew closer, the men in the cockpit could see that the base of the cloud was shot with red in places. Minutes later, the cloud resolved itself into several distinct columns, merging higher up into a single spreading pall that fanned out slowly before the easterly wind.

Stunned, the Sunderland's crew gazed down on the carnage. The sea was littered with dying ships, many of them fiercely ablaze. Dense smoke boiled up from stricken oil tankers, their shattered hulls surrounded by circles of blazing fuel in which men screamed and died. Some freighters, which must have been carrying chemical cargoes, burned with a fierce multicoloured light. The aircraft circled the remnants of the convoy slowly. The crew counted eleven vessels, either sinking or so badly damaged that it was doubtful if they could be salvaged.

The Australian squadron leader knew that convoys from Sierra Leone were provided with a light escort for the first few hundred miles of their journey; from then on they were supposed to be provided with an ocean escort, sometimes a cruiser or a battleship, but more often one of the armed merchant cruisers – converted fast liners capable of a speed of at least fifteen knots – which were no match for German warships. Ten had already been lost.

Whatever had hit this convoy, it had done so in the dangerous gap when the merchantmen were unescorted.

"Whatever did this, it wasn't a U-boat attack," the Australian said. "If it had been, there'd be ships trailing back for fifty miles. In any case, there are only half a dozen Italian boats operating in this area, and they aren't much use."

It wasn't exactly true. The Italian Admiralty had seventeen submarines operating in the area west of Biscay under the tactical command of the German Navy, and they had scored their first successes in the North Atlantic in November 1940, ranging as far afield as the waters off southern Ireland. They were a valuable addition to the German effort against the Atlantic convoys, for the German submarine service was still hampered by a lack of operational U-boats; the low priority given to submarine construction in the early part of the War – partly because the German naval planners had not expected to go to war before 1944 – meant that the Germans did not have enough craft coming off the slipways to replace the thirty-one boats lost in the first fifteen months of hostilities. There was also the German training system, which required a

U-boat crew to undergo nine months of training in the Baltic and carry out sixty-six simulated attacks before it was considered operational. The overall result was that, by the end of 1940, their operational strength stood at only twenty-two submarines. It was fortunate for Britain that this was so, because even with the depleted U-boat resources at their disposal, the Germans had come close to severing the Atlantic lifeline.

Now there was another threat, and the Sunderland captain knew that it had to involve surface warships. The question was, which ones? Not the German commerce raiders, which were operating in the Indian Ocean and the South Atlantic. Not the *Hipper*, which was still holed up in Brest; and not the *Scheer*, last seen far to the south.

Something new and deadly was out there, and it couldn't be far away. The Sunderland captain took over the controls from the young American, circled the convoy once more after instructing his wireless operator to transmit a coded signal for help, and then flew off towards the west, searching the sea.

He was going in the wrong direction. The warships that had devastated the convoy were steaming at full speed north-eastwards, towards the port of Brest.

Admiral Lutjens was reasonably content with the results of the battlecruisers' sortie into the Atlantic, which was code-named Operation Berlin; since breaking through the Denmark Strait the *Scharnhorst* and *Gneisenau* had sunk twenty-two merchant ships totalling over 115,000 tons. The total would certainly have been greater, but an attempted attack on one convoy 300 miles north-east of the Cape Verde Islands had been frustrated by the presence of a strong naval escort that included the battleship *Malaya*, and a couple of days later, while picking up survivors from a freighter, the *Gneisenau* had been surprised by the battleship HMS *Rodney*. Only the German warship's superior manoeuvrability and speed had enabled her to get away.

After attacking one more convoy, Lutjens – conscious that superior British naval forces were probably closing in on him – had ordered the captains of the *Scharnhorst* and *Gneisenau*, Hoffmann and Fein, to make independently for Brest. Also proceeding independently towards that haven were three captured oil tankers, manned by prize crews.

Lutjens was right about one thing: the Royal Navy was out in force, searching for his ships. By now, the British Admiralty was fairly certain of the identity of the warships that had been cutting a terrible swathe through the Atlantic convoys; what it did not yet know was whether the German battle group commander would turn north, heading back towards the Denmark Strait, or whether he would elect to make for one of the French Atlantic ports. It was all a big gamble, and the best the Admiralty could do was to station the limited forces at its disposal at strategic points in the hope of intercepting the enemy.

The most powerful British naval force, consisting of the battleships *Rodney*, *Nelson* and *King George V*, the cruiser *Nigeria* and two destroyers, was hurriedly sent to patrol the waters off Iceland. Another – the Gibraltar-based Force H, with the battlecruiser *Renown*, the aircraft carrier *Ark Royal*, the cruiser *Sheffield* and several destroyers, set out to patrol the waters south-west of the Bay of Biscay.

On 20 March, a Swordfish reconnaissance aircraft from the *Ark Royal* sighted two of the captured oil tankers, the *Bianca* and *San Casimiro*, its report bringing the warships racing up. They were too late to prevent the German prize crews from scuttling the vessels.

Later that day, another Swordfish located the two enemy battlecruisers, but was unable to transmit an immediate report because of wireless failure. By the time the fault was put right, any chance of intercepting the warships had vanished.

A few hours later, led by German destroyers and mine-sweepers which had put out to meet them, the *Scharnhorst* and *Gneisenau* entered the sanctuary of Brest harbour. They had it to themselves, for a couple of days earlier the *Admiral Hipper* had slipped quietly to sea and was now far out in the North Atlantic, making for the Denmark Strait. On 28 March she arrived in Kiel, having successfully evaded the British warship screen.

By that time, Admiral Lutjens was also back in Germany. Ahead of him lay the exciting challenge of a new command: he was to head a brand-new battle group spearheaded by the most powerful warship afloat. Displacing 42,500 tons and capable of twenty-eight knots, she was armed with eight 15-inch and twelve 5.9-inch guns. In just a few weeks' time, together with the heavy cruiser

Prinz Eugen and supported by supply ships and tankers, she would sail from the Baltic port of Gdynia.

The name she bore was that of the statesman who had brought Germany to a pinnacle of greatness in the nineteenth century: *Bismarck.*

Chapter Three

The Avro Anson floated over the threshold of runway one-three, its twin Cheetah engines burbling as the pilot, a young sergeant, throttled back. The main wheels screeched briefly as they touched the tarmac, then the tailwheel settled on the runway and the Anson lost speed. A metallic voice from Flying Control instructed the pilot to taxi for the airfield buildings via runway zero one. He acknowledged and looked around him, taking in the bleak surroundings. His navigator summed up his own thoughts admirably.

"What a dump! Last place God made, and it looks like he forgot to finish it."

The pilot had to admit that there was little appealing about RAF Crosby-on-Eden, tucked away in the wilds of Cumbria a few miles east of Carlisle. He had no idea, nor would he have cared if he had known, that the place was steeped in history; that his approach to land had taken him directly over the vallum of Hadrian's Wall, which ran along the aerodrome's northern boundary, and that a few yards off the Anson's starboard wingtip there was a Roman camp, on the airfield site itself.

His job did not lend itself to historical speculation.

While others were flying fighters or bombers, or hunting German U-boats, he was delivering sacks of mail around the airfields of Flying Training Command; a necessary task, but thoroughly unglamorous.

Crosby-on-Eden was the home of No. 59 Operational Training Unit. A few of its Hurricanes had arrived, but the station was far from ready to receive its full complement of aircraft. The living quarters were without electricity, there was no permanent water supply, there were no roads between the buildings, drainage was practically non-existent and telephones had only just been installed. The Anson pilot knew via the grapevine that Free French and Canadian pilots were to be trained here; he did not envy them.

The navigator, who was looking out of the starboard window, suddenly tapped the pilot on the arm, drawing his attention to something on the far side of the airfield, near some blister hangars. The pilot looked, making out some sort of angled ramp. A Hurricane sat on its lower end.

"What the blazes is that?" the navigator asked wonderingly. The pilot could only shake his head in ignorance.

A few minutes later, their mail unloaded, they were sitting in the Watch Office drinking tea with a corporal clerk. Through the grimy window, the navigator could still see the contraption on the other side of the field, and asked the corporal what it was. The corporal suddenly became very guarded.

"We don't talk about that lot," he said. "Some sort of trials outfit. Keep themselves to themselves. You might see something in a minute or two, though," he hinted.

They were not disappointed. Just as they were finishing

their tea, someone in the control tower above the Watch Office fired off a couple of red flares, warning any aircraft in the vicinity to keep clear of the aerodrome. Intrigued, the Anson crew went outside, braving the bitter wind that swept down from the Solway Firth. They were in no hurry; their aircraft had yet to be refuelled, and it would be at least half an hour before they took off on the next leg of their journey – across to Montrose, on the east coast of Scotland.

The crackling note of a Rolls-Royce Merlin reached their ears; someone had started the Hurricane's engine. After a few seconds the roar reached a crescendo as whoever was in the Hurricane's cockpit opened the throttle wide. Then something remarkable happened.

A great sheet of brilliant orange flame burst out behind the fighter, accompanied by a thunderous noise. An instant later the Hurricane shot along its ramp like a bolt fired from a crossbow, followed by the flame and a boiling horizontal column of smoke. The fighter shot off the end of the ramp, wobbled slightly, then climbed away. It turned, joined the aerodrome circuit and the pilot lowered its undercarriage in preparation for landing. Smoke from the rocket launch drifted slowly across the field.

"I wouldn't mind having a go at that," the Anson pilot said in awed tones. His navigator looked at him askance.

"Fred," he said, "your take-offs are bloody awful as it is. Forget it." He went back into the Watch Office to refill his mug. The pilot followed him slowly, wondering what the performance he had just witnessed was all about.

The Hurricane came in to land and taxied towards the blister hangars. Its pilot brought it to a stop, shut down its engine and climbed from the cockpit, nodding to the ground crew and making for a small wooden hut that served as an office and crew room. Inside, he stripped off his fleece-lined flying jacket and helmet and hung them on a convenient peg. The uniform he wore was that of a naval lieutenant commander. He poured himself some coffee from a small urn that stood precariously on a window shelf and collapsed into a nearby armchair.

"That's it, then," he said, addressing a Royal Air Force officer who sat at a table, writing furiously on a sheaf of notepaper.

Ken Armstrong laid aside his pen and stretched. On the sleeves of his blue-grey tunic he wore the three rings of a wing commander; it was a promotion that had only come through a fortnight earlier.

Armstrong glanced at Jamie Baird and nodded. He had just witnessed 'Dickie' Baird's twelfth rocket launch, and all of them had been without incident.

"Yes, that's it. There's no doubt that it works. We can go ahead and recommend it to the boys at Speke now."

Armstrong was well aware of the urgency. In the spring of 1941, the Admiralty, through a chronic shortage of aircraft carriers and a lack of suitable aircraft, had no means of defending its vital Atlantic convoys against the German long-range *Kondor* reconnaissance aircraft. Not only were they sinking substantial amounts of shipping; they were also acting as the eyes of the U-boats and warships that were loose on the high seas.

Several schemes to remedy the deficiency had been proposed; the rocket-launch technique was the one that had been chosen, and the task of proving it had been assigned to Armstrong's Special Trials and Experimental Squadron. The idea was that a number of ships ranging in size from 2,500 to 12,000 tons were to be equipped with rocket-assisted catapults and designated Catapult Aircraft Merchantmen, or CAM-ships. A number of Hurricane fighters were being fitted with catapult launch equipment. The whole operation was to be controlled by the newly-formed Merchant Ship Fighter Unit, based at Speke aerodrome near Liverpool.

Armstrong himself had made a catapult launch, although Baird had been the test pilot in charge of the project, and had found it an extraordinary experience. The rocket-powered catapult subjected aircraft and pilot to an acceleration of three and a half times the force of gravity, during which the pilot had to keep sufficient wits about him to control the Hurricane as it reached flying speed dangerously close to the stall. The technique was to use one-third starboard rudder to counteract the aircraft's tendency to swing to port, with one-third flap and the elevator and trimming tabs neutral. A further essential precaution was to jab the right elbow hard into one's hip to avoid jerking the stick, as the slightest wrong movement could cause the aircraft to fall out of the sky during the critical launch phase.

The trials were complete now, and operational training at Speke could begin. The call for volunteers had already gone out, and a surprising number of pilots had come forward, both from the RAF and the Fleet Air Arm. Armstrong did not envy their task; their only alternatives, after being launched on a combat mission out of range of land, would be to bale out or to ditch the aircraft as close as possible to the convoy they were protecting, in the hope of being picked up before the icy Atlantic seas claimed them.

Proving the rocket-launched fighter concept had been the latest task given to Armstrong's squadron. Officially, the squadron did not exist: it had no number, no regular base. Since it had been formed in 1940 on the orders of Air Chief Marshal Sir Hugh Dowding, the Commander-in-Chief of RAF Fighter Command, it had accomplished a variety of tasks – including the pioneering of intruder operations over enemy-occupied Europe and the development of night-fighting techniques – and had led a nomadic existence. But it had expanded into something much larger than an ordinary RAF squadron, which explained Armstrong's rise in rank, and there were parts of it scattered all over the British Isles. The lack of centralisation was essential from the security point of view; if it were concentrated in one place, German Intelligence would be sure to learn of its existence, and once that happened the Germans would soon establish its purpose.

The task of Armstrong and his 'secret squadron' was simple. It was to devise ways and means of taking the war to the enemy, using whatever technology was available. Its reponsibility was to the Chiefs of Staff, and through them to the Prime Minister himself. The authority of Winston Churchill was stamped on all its activities, which had enabled Armstrong to cut through a lot of red tape. Inevitably, he had made a few enemies en route, usually among desk-bound officers who viewed with horror any procedure that circumvented the 'usual channels'.

Acting in support of the Admiralty and its endeavours to

keep Britain's lifelines open was now the squadron's priority task, for these were desperate times. The Battle of Britain had been fought and won, but although the immediate danger of invasion had receded Britain stood alone, facing an implacable and ruthless enemy who controlled all of Europe's coastline from Norway's North Cape to the Bay of Biscay.

Only the RAF was in a position to strike at the enemy-held ports, but in the early months of 1941 its resources were still pitifully weak, and results so far had been negligible. The first of Bomber Command's new heavy bombers, the Short Stirling, had flown its first operational mission on the night of 10 February, three aircraft of No. 7 Squadron from Oakington taking part in an attack on the oil storage tanks at Rotterdam, and on 10 March six Handley Page Halifaxes of No. 35 Squadron had been sent out to bomb Le Havre dockyard. Four bombed the primary target, one attacked Dieppe, and one aborted. It was hardly a successful mission, and to make matters worse one of the Halifaxes was shot down by an RAF night fighter over Surrey while returning to base.

The third new heavy bomber to enter service, the Avro Manchester, was a bitter disappointment to Bomber Command. It was designed to the same specification as the Halifax, but used two Rolls-Royce Vulture engines instead of four Merlins, with unfortunate consequences. On the night of 24 February 1941, six aircraft of No. 207 Squadron set out to attack Brest harbour, and one crashed through engine failure on its return. The Vulture engines were unreliable; often, they would carry the aircraft on long-distance raids without the slightest hint of trouble, only to burst into flames for no apparent reason towards the end of the sortie. To solve the problem, Avro had been experimenting with a converted Manchester, known as the Mark III, fitted with four Merlins. The aircraft had made its first flight in January 1941, and it had now received a new name. They called it the Lancaster.

At Crosby-on-Eden, the light was fading fast, and Armstrong decided to call it a day. After making sure that everything was secure and telling the ground staff to go off for their tea, he and Baird headed for the latter's car. Armstrong and his staff had arrived at Crosby some five weeks before, while the living accommodation on the airfield was still being erected; he had fixed up a billet for the officers in a small hotel in the village of Brampton, about three miles away, and for the other ranks in a comfortable youth hostel that was normally used by the hikers who had trudged along the Roman Wall in happier times. Armstrong liked the arrangement, which did away with the need to use the messes on the aerodrome and preserved a great deal of his unit's anonymity. The squadron personnel all had the benefit of a good breakfast and dinner, and sandwiches took care of their lunch requirement.

The little hotel in Brampton was run by a charming middle-aged couple, the MacDonalds, who did not in the least mind being overwhelmed by Service officers. After all, they paid the bills in a time of hardship. Armstrong and Baird made straight for the residents' lounge where, as they had predicted, a cheerful fire was burning. Beside it, in a high-backed chair, a man sat, and in contrast to the fire he looked anything but cheerful. He wore grey slacks, a thick white pullover and carpet slippers, and as the two officers entered the room he was busily and noisily applying a handkerchief to a nose that was a deep shade of red.

"Feeling any better, Stan?" Armstrong enquired, sitting down opposite and stretching out his hands towards the blaze. Flight Lieutenant Stanislaw Kalinski peered miserably at him through streaming eyes.

"No," the Polish officer said bluntly. "And I think I've been poisoned." He explained that Mrs MacDonald had been dosing him heavily with her own patent cold cure. "A few brandies would fix me," he added, "but there's not much chance of that here, is there?"

Baird, who was sitting astride a dining chair, his arms resting on its back, gave a barely suppressed snort of laughter. Kalinski's love of strong liquor was well known, and his face when he found out that Armstrong had billeted them in a temperance hotel had been something to behold.

Kalinski's cold was the result, or so he claimed, of a brief flirtation with one of the RAF's twin-engined medium bombers, the Handley Page Hampden. One Hampden squadron, based in East Anglia, had been given the task of carrying out torpedo-dropping trials with the aircraft, and Kalinski had been despatched to observe and report back on the success or otherwise of the scheme. The trials had been carried out over a bombing range in The Wash; since the Hampden was designed to be flown by only one pilot, Kalinski had made a number of trips over a period of about a week in the upper gun position to watch results, and had quickly discovered one of the Hampden's limitations. The bomber was very streamlined, and as the airflow swept past

23

its narrow fuselage sides it curved in behind the gun turret and sent a backwash of icy air through the gap in the cupola through which the machine-guns protruded. After each trip, Kalinski had crawled from the turret frozen stiff, with a layer of ice crackling on his face.

As soon as his cold had developed after his return, Armstrong had confined him to quarters, despite the Pole's protests.

"You know the score, Stan," he had told him. "You'd only give it to everyone else, and people can't fly with a cold. Stay in the warm and write up your report instead." Which is exactly what Kalinski had done, grumbling under his breath about the lack of fortifying drink.

Their host, a portly man with a tonsure of grey hair and a chubby, florid face, came in and greeted them warmly in a strong Cumbrian accent.

"Dinner will be ready shortly," he announced. "Mrs Mac has some nice mutton stew on the go. Just the ticket for a cold night." He stooped over the hearth, picked up the coal scuttle and threw some of its contents on the fire. "Must listen to the nine o'clock news tonight," he said, straightening up. "Maybe there'll be more about that naval victory in the Med."

"What victory's that, Mr Mac?" Armstrong wanted to know. MacDonald turned his ruddy features towards him.

"There's been a battle," he said. "It was mentioned on the six o'clock bulletin. Our lads have given the Eyeties another pasting. Almost as good as Taranto, they reckon."

Taranto, Armstrong reflected, following hard on the heels of the RAF's hard-won victory over southern England last summer, had provided a real tonic for British morale, and a superb effort on the part of the British Mediterranean Fleet. At one stroke, it had knocked out the most dangerous and effective units of the Italian Fleet. Armstrong had made a careful study of the action, for there were many lessons to be learned from it.

Plans for an attack on Taranto by carrier-borne aircraft had been laid as long ago as 1935, when Italian forces invaded Abyssinia. There were actually two main Italian naval bases, one at Naples and the other at Taranto; and it was at the latter, in the autumn of 1940, that the Italians had begun to concentrate their heavy naval units to counter the threat from the British Mediterranean Fleet.

With only the old carrier *Eagle* at the disposal of the British naval commander, Admiral Cunningham, an attack on the big Italian base had been regarded as impracticable, but the arrival of the much more modern *Illustrious* by way of reinforcement had changed the picture completely. The plans were revised, and it was decided to mount a strike from the *Illustrious* and *Eagle* on the night of 21 October, the anniversary of the Battle of Trafalgar. Before that date, however, a serious fire swept through *Illustrious*'s hangar; some of her aircraft were totally destroyed and others put temporarily out of action, and the strike had to be postponed by three weeks.

Air reconnaissance had revealed that five of the six battle-ships of the Italian battle fleet were at Taranto, as well as a large force of cruisers and destroyers. The battleships and some of the cruisers were moored in the outer harbour, the Mar Grande, a horseshoe-shaped expanse of fairly shallow water, while the other cruisers and destroyers lay in the inner harbour, the Mar Piccolo. The ships in the outer harbour were protected by torpedo nets and lines of barrage balloons. It was the balloons, perhaps even more than the anti-aircraft batteries, that would present the greatest hazard to the low-flying Swordfish.

The date of the attack – code-named Operation Judgement – was fixed for the night of 11 November. Because of defects caused by the many near-misses she had suffered in earlier air attacks, the *Eagle* had to be withdrawn from the operation at the last moment; five of her aircraft were transferred to the other carrier. The *Illustrious* and the fleet sailed from Alexandria on 6 November, and two days later the warships made rendezvous with several military convoys in the Ionian Sea, on their way from Malta to Alexandria and Greece. The concentration of ships was located and attacked by the *Regia Aeronautica*, the Italian Air Force, during the next two days, but the attacks were broken up by 806 Squadron's Fulmar fighters, which claimed the destruction of ten enemy aircraft for no loss.

At 1800 on the 11th, with the convoys safely on their way under escort, the *Illustrious*, with a screen of four cruisers and four destroyers, detached herself from the main force and headed for her flying-off position 170 miles from Taranto. Twenty-one aircraft were available for the strike: twelve from 815 Squadron, led by Lieutenant Commander Ken Williamson, and nine from No. 819 under Lieutenant Commander 'Ginger' Hale. Because of the restricted space available over the target, only six aircraft from each wave were to carry torpedoes; the others were to drop flares to the east of the Mar Grande, silhouetting the warships anchored there, or to dive-bomb the vessels in the Mar Piccolo.

The first wave of Swordfish began taking off at 2040 and set course in clear weather, climbing to 8,000 feet and reaching the enemy coast at 2220. The Swordfish formation then split in two, the torpedo-carriers turning away to make their approach from the west while the flare-droppers headed for a point east of the Mar Grande. At 2300 the torpedo aircraft were in position and began their attack, diving in line astern with engines throttled well back. Williamson, descending to thirty feet, passed over the stern of the battleship *Diga di Tarantola* and released his torpedo at the destroyer *Fulmine*; it missed and ran on to explode against the side of a bigger target, the battleship *Conte di Cavour*. Then the Swordfish was hit by AA fire and had to ditch; Williamson and his observer, Lieutenant Scarlett, were taken prisoner. Two torpedoes from the remaining Swordfish hit the brand-new battleship *Littorio*; the aircraft all got clear of the target area and set course for the carrier. So did the other six Swordfish, whose bombs had damaged some oil tanks and started a big fire in the seaplane base beside the Mar Piccolo.

The second wave, which had taken off some fifty minutes after the first, had no difficulty in locating Taranto; the whole target area was lit up by searchlights and the glare of fires. There were only eight aircraft in this wave – the ninth had been forced to turn back to the carrier with mechanical trouble. This time, the five torpedo-carriers came in from the north. Two of their torpedoes hit the *Littorio* and another the *Caio Duilio*; a fourth narrowly missed the *Vittorio Veneto*.

The fifth Swordfish was hit and exploded, killing both crew members.

By 0300 all the surviving Swordfish had been recovered safely, although some had substantial battle damage. Some of the crews who had bombed the vessels in the Mar Piccolo reported that some bombs had failed to explode; one had hit the cruiser *Trento* amidships, only to bounce off into the water, and the same had happened with a hit on the destroyer *Libeccio*.

The following day, RAF reconnaissance photographs told the full story of the damage inflicted on the Italian Fleet. The mighty *Littorio*, with great gaps torn in her side by three torpedoes, was badly down by the bow and leaking huge quantities of oil; it would take four months to effect repairs. The *Caio Duilio* and the *Conte di Cavour* had taken one hit each; the former had been beached and the latter had sunk on the bottom.

Armstrong was not the only one who had analysed the Taranto attack with great interest. On the other side of the world, another man had made a careful study of it, thinking: if the British could achieve such a result with a handful of outdated biplanes, what might be achieved with a large force of modern dive-bombers and torpedo-bombers against a fleet in harbour? The blueprint for just such an attack was already being drawn up by Admiral Isoroku Yamamoto of the Imperial Japanese Navy, whose country was not yet at war with the powerful nations of the West.

It was four months since Taranto, and in the meantime the Mediterranean Fleet had suffered some severe reverses, for a new power had intervened in the Mediterranean war. It should not have come as a surprise to the British.

On 9 January 1941 a convoy of four big supply ships, escorted by HMS *Ark Royal* and the other warships of Force H, entered the narrows between Sicily and Tunis on its way to Malta and Piraeus. The passage of the ships through the troubled waters of the central Mediterranean – known as Operation Excess – at first followed the pattern of earlier convoys. In the afternoon of the 9th the usual formation of Italian Savoia SM79s appeared and bombed from high altitude without scoring any hits; two of the SM79s were intercepted by *Ark Royal*'s Fulmars and shot down.

As darkness fell, Force H turned back towards Gibraltar, leaving the cruiser *Bonaventure* and the destroyers *Jaguar, Hereward, Hasty* and *Hero* to shepherd the convoy through the narrows under cover of night. At dawn on the 10th, the transports were met by the ships of the Eastern Mediterranean Fleet, comprising the carrier *Illustrious*, the battleships *Warspite* and *Valiant* and seven destroyers sixty miles west of Malta. Admiral Cunningham's ships had already suffered; shortly before first light, the destroyer *Gallant* had been badly damaged by a mine and had to be taken in tow by HMS *Mohawk*.

Torpedo attacks by ten SM79s were beaten off in the course of the morning, and the Italian MTB *Vega* was sunk by the *Bonaventure*. Then *Illustrious*'s radar detected another incoming formation of enemy aircraft, which soon afterwards was sighted approaching the warships at 12,000 feet. Sailors who had fought in the waters off Norway and

Dunkirk recognised the enemy aircraft at once; they were Junkers Ju 87 dive-bombers.

The *Stukas* were the aircraft of StG1 and StG2, led by *Hauptmann* Werner Hozzel and *Major* Walter Enneccerus. They formed the mainstay of the *Luftwaffe*'s special anti-shipping formation, *Fliegerkorps* X, and they had arrived at Trapani in Sicily less than a week earlier. Their presence should not have come as a surprise; Air Ministry Intelligence had been aware since 4 January of *Fliegerkorps* X's move south from Norway, and it was also aware of the unit's specialised role. The threat to the Mediterranean Fleet was clear; unfortunately, at this point there was a breakdown in communication between the Air Ministry and the Admiralty, and the *Stukas* came as an unpleasant shock. Now, as they began their attack dive, it was clear that they had singled out *Illustrious* as their principal target. The first bomb tore through S1 pom-pom on the carrier's port side, reducing the weapon to twisted wreckage and killing two of its crew before passing through the platform and exploding in the sea. Another bomb exploded on S2 pom-pom and obliterated it, together with its crew. A third hit the after-well lift, on its way to the flight deck with a Fulmar on it; debris and burning fuel poured into the hangar below, which quickly became an inferno of blazing aircraft and exploding fuel tanks. Splinters struck the eight 4.5-inch gun turrets aft, putting them all out of action. A fourth bomb crashed through the flight deck and ripped through the ship's side, exploding in the water; splinters punched holes through the hull and the shock of the detonation caused more damage in the hangar. The fifth bomb punched through the flight deck and hangar deck and exploded in the wardroom flat, killing everyone there and sending a storm of fire raging through the neighbouring passages. A sixth plunged down the after-lift well and exploded in the compartment below, putting the steering-gear out of action.

Illustrious was terribly hurt, but her heavy armour had saved her. Slowly the crew gained a measure of control and she turned towards Malta, shrouded in a pall of smoke from the fires that still raged, steering on her main engines as the stokers worked in dense, choking fumes and temperatures reaching 140°F as they strove to maintain steam. Two hours later the *Stukas* attacked again and the carrier was hit by yet another bomb; she was now listing badly, but she remained afloat. As darkness fell, she limped into Valletta's Grand Harbour and stopped alongside the dockyard wall.

During the weeks that followed, *Illustrious* sustained several more bomb hits as she underwent repairs, but she escaped crippling damage and by 23 January she had been made seaworthy enough to sail for Alexandria. From there she later sailed for the US Navy shipyards at Norfolk, Virginia, where she underwent more permanent repairs before returning to active service.

As they listened to the BBC news in the warmth of the little hotel on this last day of March, 1941, Armstrong and his colleagues became aware that the Royal Navy had once again provided a bright glow in a picture that was otherwise gloomy. There had been a military coup in Yugoslavia; the young heir to the throne, Peter, had been declared king, and pro-German factions expelled from the country.

"The Germans won't stand for it," Kalinski said gloomily.

"They are already massing an army in Romania. They will soon invade Yugoslavia and Greece, depend upon it."

"But why?" Baird wanted to know. "What advantage would they gain from that?"

"The advantage, my friend," Kalinski said, "lies in securing their southern flank. I believe that the Germans are planning an attack on the Soviet Union."

"Surely they wouldn't be that stupid," Mr MacDonald said. "Nobody has ever invaded Russia and succeeded. What if—"

He was interrupted by the measured tones of John Snagge, the newsreader, giving details of the fleet action in the Mediterranean. They listened in silence as Snagge intoned the story of what had undoubtedly been a resounding victory; but the three officers in the room were all sharing the same thoughts. If Kalinski was right, then the *Luftwaffe* would soon be operating in the Mediterranean in strength, and then the Navy would have a fight on its hands.

Interlude: Cape Matapan – 28 March 1941

On 9 March 1941, the gap created by the absence of HMS *Illustrious* was filled when HMS *Formidable*, her sister carrier, joined the Mediterranean Fleet. She carried only four Swordfish; the rest of her aircraft complement was made up of ten Fairey Albacores – biplanes, like the Swordfish, but bigger and faster, with a longer range and an enclosed cockpit – of No. 826 Squadron, and the thirteen Fulmars of No. 803 Squadron, transferred from the *Ark Royal*. The fighter complement would be brought up to full strength in the following month, when No. 806 Squadron joined the carrier from Malta. Before that, however, *Formidable* and her aircraft were to play a decisive part in another large-scale action against the Italian Fleet.

At dawn on 28 March, while the Mediterranean Fleet was engaged in covering the passage of convoys of British Commonwealth troops from Alexandria to Greece to counter a highly probable German invasion of that country, a reconnaissance Albacore from the *Formidable* reported a force of enemy cruisers and destroyers to the south of Crete. This force, which actually comprised the battleship *Vittorio Veneto* – the flagship of the Italian commander, Admiral Iachino – six heavy cruisers, two light cruisers and thirteen destroyers, had put to sea from Taranto, Naples, Brindisi and Messina and had made rendezvous south of the Straits of Messina on 27 March with the object of intercepting the British troop convoys. Iachino had agreed to the operation only when the *Luftwaffe* promised him extensive fighter cover and reconnaissance facilities, and after the crews of two Heinkel 111 torpedo bombers had erroneously reported hits on two large warships – 'possibly battleships' – during an armed reconnaissance flight thirty nautical miles west of Crete on 16 March. It was a mistake that was to have serious consequences for the Italian admiral.

At 0815 on 28 March the Mediterranean Fleet's cruisers, which were about 100 miles ahead of the main force, came under fire from the Italian warships and were in danger of being cut off by the enemy, who was steaming in a large pincer formation. With no hope of Admiral Cunningham's heavy brigade arriving in time to ease the situation, it was apparent that only a torpedo strike by *Formidable*'s aircraft could ease the pressure on the outgunned British cruisers, and at 1000 six Albacores – the only ones available, as the other four were earmarked for reconnaissance duties – took off with an escort of two Fulmars and headed for the Italian squadrons. Their orders were to attack the enemy cruisers, but the first ship they sighted was the *Vittorio Veneto*, whose 15-inch guns were pounding the British cruiser squadron. The Fleet Air Arm pilots attacked in two waves at 1125, but the Italian battleship took evasive action and all the torpedoes missed. The two Fulmars, meanwhile, had engaged two Ju 88s high overhead and destroyed one of them, driving the other off.

Admiral Iachino, seeing his air cover melt away, now turned away and headed west at speed, reducing Cunningham's hopes of bringing him to action. The British commander ordered a second air strike, this time with the object of slowing down the *Vittorio Veneto*, and the *Formidable* accordingly flew off three Albacores and two Swordfish, again escorted by a pair of Fulmars. They sighted their target – which had meanwhile been unsuccessfully attacked by RAF Blenheim bombers from bases in Greece – an hour later. This time, mainly because they were on the alert for more RAF aircraft approaching from a different direction, the Italian gunners failed to see the Fleet Air Arm aircraft until the latter began their attack. The Albacores came in first, led by Lieutenant Commander Dalyell-Stead; he released his torpedo seconds before his aircraft was hit and blew up. The torpedo ran true and exploded on the battleship's stern, jamming her steering gear and flooding the compartment with 4,000 tons of water. No further torpedo hits were registered, but the *Vittorio Veneto* was forced to slow down and stop while her engineers made temporary repairs, spurred by the knowledge that Cunningham's battleships were now only three hours' steaming time away. They succeeded in repairing the propeller shaft and gradually the battleship's speed was worked up until she was able to proceed at between fifteen and eighteen knots, with the cruisers and destroyers forming a tight screen around her.

The *Formidable*'s third and last attack was launched at dusk. Led by Lieutenant Commander W.H.G. Saunt, six Albacores and four Swordfish, two of the latter from Maleme airfield on Crete, caught up with the damaged battleship and her escort and attacked through heavy AA fire. The *Vittorio Veneto* escaped further harm, but one torpedo heading for the battleship was blocked by the cruiser *Pola*, which was badly damaged. Admiral Iachino detached the cruisers *Zara* and *Fiume* and four destroyers to escort her, while the rest of the Italian force accompanied the *Vittorio Veneto* to safety.

At 2210 the three cruisers and the destroyers were detected by radar on board the battleship HMS *Valiant* and the cruiser *Orion*. Fifteen minutes later the Italian ships were engaged by *Valiant* and *Warspite* and the *Zara* and *Fiume* were quickly reduced to blazing hulks; two destroyers were sent in to finish them off with torpedoes. The crippled *Pola* was also sunk before morning, as well as two of the Italian destroyers. The enemy warships, which were not equipped with radar, had no idea that they were steaming across the bows of the British force until the battleships opened fire on them.

The Italians had lost five warships and nearly 2,500 officers and men; the British had lost just one Albacore. So ended the action that was to become known as the Battle of Cape Matapan.

Chapter Four

Eastchurch Airfield, Kent – 3 April 1941

Of all the aircraft that might have been allocated to him as
his personal transport, Armstrong could not have wished for
anything better than the North American Harvard advanced
trainer. A low-wing, two-seat aircraft, the Harvard would
cruise happily at 150 m.p.h., making it ideal for liaison
between the airfields over which the various flights of
Armstrong's squadron were scattered. The front cockpit
was ideal – neither too roomy nor too cramped, with
all the switches and levers in easy reach and with excellent visibility; the rear cockpit, normally occupied by an
instructor but now occupied by Dickie Baird, was almost
as good, if somewhat more stark.

In the cockpit, with the canopy closed, the noise of the
big 600 horsepower Pratt and Whitney Wasp radial engine
was muted, but to anyone outside it produced a fearful
racket, a blare caused by the tips of the propeller blades
exceeding supersonic speed. The engine produced plenty
of power for everything, from providing good acceleration
on take-off to performing continuous aerobatics without
losing height. Armstrong loved it, and had to be politely

reminded from time to time by his colleagues that the aircraft was actually assigned to the squadron, and not to him personally. He took absolutely no notice.

Eastchurch aerodrome, on the Isle of Sheppey, had taken a fearful battering during the Battle of Britain and had not been much used since, which suited Armstrong very well. The squadron's 'B' Flight, with four cannon-armed Hurricanes, was based here under the command of Flying Officer Piet Van Berg, a South African who had been commissioned a few months earlier. Armstrong could see a couple of the Hurricanes as he circled the airfield prior to landing, still bearing the black paint that had been sprayed on them to conform with their night-fighter activities the previous winter.

Their task was different now. For some weeks, Van Berg and his small band of pilots had been assessing the cannon-armed Hurricane as a possible anti-shipping weapon, making sporadic attacks on the enemy maritime traffic that plied along the enemy-held Channel coast. Two of the aircraft had been equipped to carry a pair of 250-pound bombs, and trials with these had just started. The trials were in connection with a combined operation called Channel Stop, which had recently been launched by the Admiralty and the RAF and which was intended to close the English Channel to enemy shipping.

The task should have been assigned to RAF Coastal Command, but because Coastal was short of aircraft the job had been given to the Blenheim squadrons of Bomber Command's No. 2 Group, which flew regular armed reconnaissance sorties, known as 'beats', off the coasts of Holland, Belgium and northern France. The bombers flew at low level in a rectangular pattern towards, along and finally away from the enemy coastline; the idea was to surprise enemy shipping by attacking from the landward side, and was also calculated to be the best tactic to avoid interception by enemy fighter patrols. But the increasing use of flak ships attached to the German convoys, coupled with the inherent risks of low-level operations and the ability of the *Luftwaffe* to mount effective convoy protection patrols, resulted in appalling losses; about 25 per cent of the Blenheims that set out never came back.

Armstrong brought the Harvard down to land and taxied towards an intact hangar, which served as accommodation for the Hurricanes and an office for the 'B' Flight staff, who were quartered in a nearby village. They climbed from the cockpit and jumped from the wing as a couple of ground crew hurried to place chocks in front of the wheels, then strolled towards the hangar over grass that was soaking wet from a recent shower. A fresh breeze came from the south-west, bringing a tang of salt air with it.

A few minutes later they were sitting in Van Berg's office, drinking welcome mugs of tea and eating bacon sandwiches that an airman had produced. Equally as welcome was a warm shaft of morning sunlight that streamed through the window. Armstrong automatically glanced at his watch; it was ten-thirty.

"So, Piet, what progress so far?" Armstrong asked through a mouthful of food.

"Mixed fortunes, sir," the South African told him. "Bomb trials so far against static ground targets have been okay; there have been no problems with bomb release, the aircraft is a stable platform and we've produced some reasonable results in shallow diving attacks. It's been a different tale, though, when we've tried the same tactics against splash targets towed by motor launches at sea. Up to now, we haven't managed to hit a damn thing. Can't seem to get the angle right. So we're going to try something else this morning. We'll motor out to Leysdown when you've finished your sandwiches."

A gunnery and bombing range had been set up during the inter-war years on the north-east shore of the Isle of Sheppey, near Leysdown. They reached it along a narrow road that ran through marshland. Van Berg halted the car at a vantage point overlooking the sea and handed a pair of binoculars to Armstrong, pointing.

"If you look over there, sir, about a mile offshore, you'll see an oblong wood-and-canvas structure which we've rigged up on some pontoons. It's got the same dimensions as the side of a small freighter, near as dammit. There will now be a short delay," he added theatrically, "before the proceedings start. Let's get out and take a good look. There are a couple of spare pairs of glasses on the back seat."

They stood out in the open for several minutes. The wind was keen and Armstrong and Baird were glad of their flying jackets. At last, they heard the song of a Rolls-Royce Merlin engine.

Looking in the direction of the sound, they saw a

black-painted Hurricane crossing the shoreline. Armstrong raised his binoculars and, as the aircraft levelled out, he saw that it had a bomb under each wing. It came down until it was very low, flying at high speed over the water. It headed straight for the target, still at a height of only a few feet. At a range of 200 yards or so the pilot released his pair of bombs and at the same instant pulled back hard on the stick, sending the Hurricane rocketing skywards.

His interest quickening, Armstrong kept his glasses focused on the two bombs, which continued to travel forwards in a flat trajectory for a few seconds. They hit the water and, to his amazement, bounced back into the air again. Travelling forwards once more, their velocity undiminished, they skipped directly over the target and bounded across the sea in a series of splashes before sinking out of sight.

The Hurricane circled overhead, waggling its wings, and headed back towards Eastchurch, the pilot lowering his undercarriage as he descended.

"Well, I'll be blowed!" Dickie Baird exclaimed, with memories of skimming flat stones over the surface of a pond as a child. "Ducks and drakes!"

Van Berg grinned. "Not quite," he pointed out. "But the principle is the same. And it has one big advantage: the attacking aircraft doesn't need to fly over the ship. If we had something faster than the Hurricane, the weapons could be released at a greater distance. It's all pretty rudimentary at the moment, but I reckon that if that target had been a stationary ship, the bombs would have hit the superstructure. Anyway, you've seen what I wanted you to see; now we'll go and have a word with

Nick Pitchford, the pilot. It was his idea, as a matter of fact."

It had been Baird's idea to recruit Sub Lieutenant Pitchford into the special duties squadron; he had been one of Pitchford's instructors earlier in the War, and had been impressed by the young pilot's ability. Armstrong's attitude to his deputy's original suggestion had been sanguine; he didn't much care where his pilots came from, so long as they were better than average and were capable of tackling a variety of difficult and dangerous jobs.

Three-quarters of an hour later they were back in Van Berg's office at Eastchurch, in deep conversation with Pitchford, a lanky individual with a lopsided smile and fair hair which, in Armstrong's opinion, sorely needed the attention of a barber. Armstrong wanted to know how the young naval officer had stumbled on the idea of the skip-bombing technique, as Pitchford called it.

"Actually, sir, it was Sir Francis Drake's idea in the first place, or if it wasn't him, he was the first one to put it into practice. Even before the Spanish Armada set sail, Drake knew that his little ships would have to get in really close to the Spaniards if their twenty-five pounder guns were to make much impression on the galleons, which meant that they would have to run the gauntlet of heavy fire on the way and possibly get themselves sunk before they came within range. So Drake developed a technique of bouncing his roundshot off the surface of the sea, which made it spin and gave it not only extra range but also extra velocity and therefore more penetrating power. Another advantage was that a ricochet off the sea would strike an enemy ship in an upward trajectory, causing damage to masts and rigging. That's how most ships were disabled in the days of sail; very few were actually sunk by direct gunfire."

"So you think the idea is really workable?" Armstrong asked him. "I mean – notwithstanding the trial we saw this morning – is it feasible to expect bombs to bounce off the sea and hit a moving target?"

Pitchford frowned, shaking his head slowly. "Not without redesigning them, I don't think," he said. "They tend to wobble after the ricochet and go badly off trajectory. What's needed, to my mind, is a spherical bomb, like the old cannonball, and it needs to be spinning before it hits the water. In that way it would keep more or less straight – straight enough to hit a target the size of a ship, anyway."

"Well, the idea's certainly worth developing further," Armstrong said. "We'll put it up to the research and development people at the Ministry. Any other comments?"

Van Berg cleared his throat. "Well, sir, what about an anti-shipping bomb that's powered by a rocket motor?"

The others stared at him. "Rocket motor?" Armstrong queried. The South African nodded. "That's right, sir. It's a notion that's been rattling around inside my head for some time. Let me show you."

He went over to a filing cabinet, unlocked one of its drawers, flicked his way through some buff folders and eventually picked one out. He placed it on his desk top and opened it, turning it around so that Armstrong could see its contents. Armstrong studied them; they were cuttings from various aviation magazines, some in foreign languages, and they were all to do with the Russian Air Force, about which Armstrong knew next to nothing. He raised his eyebrows and looked at Van Berg.

"Well, Piet? What's your point?"

"The point, sir," Van Berg explained patiently, "is this. All these articles deal with the Russians' use of rockets during their border dispute with the Japanese a couple of years ago. If you remember, there was quite a bit of fighting between the Japs in Manchuria and the Russians over some strip of territory."

Armstrong didn't, but let the point pass and studied the clippings more closely. Every one contained references to the use of air-to-ground rockets, and on one occasion Russian pilots were even said to have shot down a couple of Japanese aircraft by firing rocket projectiles at them.

"Well," Armstrong said at length, "I'll agree it's a useful idea, and the Russians seem to place a lot of reliance on it, but as far as I'm aware we've done no rocket research work at all, and even if we were to start now it would be a long time before we could turn rockets into viable weapons. And time is something we don't have. We'll add rockets to the list of recommendations, though. You never know – something might come of it. By the way, Piet, how on earth did you come by all these press cuttings?"

The South African grinned and tapped the side of his nose with his index finger.

"A cousin of mine in Switzerland," he said. "He's a sensible type; deals in diamonds. He's in touch with the folks at home, and he sends them stuff he thinks might interest me. We've been corresponding since we were kids.

He's always been keen on aeroplanes. Does a fair bit of gliding himself, and reads all the flying magazines. They get all of 'em over there, apparently, including the German ones. After all, the Swiss are neutral, aren't they?"

Armstrong smiled. It was true, of course; but he knew perfectly well that the Swiss, like the neutral Portuguese and Swedes, sympathised with the Allies. An enormous amount of intelligence reached Britain through the diplomatic channels of all three countries.

"Nick and I paid a visit to the Coastal Forces boys at Felixstowe the other day," Van Berg announced suddenly. "Thought we might be able to work out some joint tactics with them. Everything's a bit hit or miss, at the moment."

In the winter of 1940–1, attacks on British coastal convoys by enemy fast attack craft – *Schnellboote*, which the British erroneously called E-Boats – had presented a serious threat, and in an attempt to counter it the Admiralty had formed the 6th Motor Gunboat Flotilla. It consisted of three previously converted boats, armed with four Lewis guns and one Oerlikon, and five boats originally built for the French Navy; these were armed with four Lewis guns and four .303-inch Browing machine-guns in a power-operated turret. The 6th MGB Flotilla had deployed to Felixstowe early in March and had gone into action immediately, patrolling the North Sea from the Humber to the Hook of Holland and from Texel to the Thames. A couple of Motor Torpedo Boat flotillas also operated out of Felixstowe and Lowestoft; as well as their torpedoes, the MTBs were armed with a two-pounder

Rolls gun – popularly known as a pom-pom – twin 20-mm Oerlikon cannon and a Vickers machine-gun.

While the MGBs searched for prowling E-Boats, Van Berg explained, the MTBs carried out sweeps along the Dutch coast from the Hook of Holland to Den Helder. These sweeps generally consisted of seven or eight boats, their crews briefed simply to attack any enemy ships they encountered.

"They're brave beggars," Van Berg admitted. "The night before our visit, two MGBs apparently tacked themselves on to the tail of about seventeen E-Boats that were lining up to enter Ijmuiden harbour. They went down the line, shooting up as many as possible, and got away with it somehow. They haven't had much success against enemy shipping as yet, though. Seems there are problems; for instance, targets are difficult to distinguish in the dark, and if you shine a searchlight on to them to make a positive identification you become a target yourself. So Nick and I had a bit of a think, and we might have come up with something."

The South African paused, collecting his thoughts, then went on:

"What if, every time the Coastal Forces go out to take a crack at enemy shipping, we have a flight of Hurricanes standing by, armed with bombs, at a coastal airfield, ready to go? And what if the Swordfish boys at Manston go out ahead of the boats to make a reconnaissance? It would be much easier to spot an enemy convoy from the air, and once it was sighted the Swordfish could get between it and the land and drop a pattern of flares, so that the ships would be nicely silhouetted. Radio communication between the boats and the Swordfish wouldn't be a problem, because they use the same type of wireless set. The Hurricanes don't, so they would have to be alerted for take-off by Manston, who would be listening in and who would get a call through to wherever the Hurricanes were positioned. With their speed, they'd be at the scene in no time."

Armstrong shook his head. "Somehow, I don't think the Fleet Air Arm chaps at Manston would be too keen on the idea," he objected. "After all, the Swordfish would be sitting ducks, lit up by their own flares."

"As a matter of fact, sir," Pitchford interjected, "the Fleet Air Arm think it's quite a good scheme. We've already had a chat with the boss at Manston. After all, the Swordfish have been stooging around over places like Boulogne for months, dropping flares and bombs, and haven't come to grief. And the flak over the ships is likely to be a good deal less than the flak over the harbours."

"So, with your approval, we'd like to give it a try," Van Berg said, smiling at Armstrong.

"All right, then," the latter conceded. "Just don't bend anything, that's all. And I shall want a very full report." He sighed. "As a matter of fact, things are moving far too slowly for my taste. Anything that helps to take us on to the offensive is worth trying. Those bastards have had it all their own way for far to long."

The RAF had already taken the lead in going over to the offensive. Bomber Command's night attacks on Germany were increasing, although as yet they were producing little result; but Fighter Command, superb in defence during the critical Battle of Britain, was now also taking the war to the enemy.

It had started in a very small way on 20 December 1940, when two Spitfire pilots of No. 66 Squadron had taken off from Biggin Hill, crossed the Channel at low level and attacked Le Touquet airfield. During the next few days, Spitfires and Hurricanes from other squadrons, operating in twos and threes, also made short dashes into enemy-occupied territory; their pilots reported no sign of German aircraft in the air. Encouraged, Fighter Command decided to try something bigger, and on 9 January 1941, in brilliant sunshine and perfect visibility, five fighter squadrons penetrated thirty miles into France. There was no sign of movement on the snow-covered airfields they flew over; not a single Messerschmitt took to the air to intercept them.

The following day, the RAF decided to stir up a hornets' nest. In the morning, six Blenheims of No. 114 Squadron, escorted by six squadrons of Hurricanes and Spitfires, attacked ammunition and stores dumps inside France. This time, the *Luftwaffe* took the bait, but only to a limited extent. There was some skirmishing, in the course of which one Hurricane was shot down; two battle-damaged Spitfires crash-landed on return to base, one of the pilots being killed.

By March 1941, in the face of growing enemy opposition, fighter sweeps over France – known as 'Circuses' – were becoming organised affairs, with the Spitfire and Hurricane squadrons operating in Wing strength. A

Fighter Command Wing consisted of three squadrons, each of twelve aircraft. There were Spitfire Wings at Biggin Hill, Hornchurch and Tangmere, mixed Spitfire and Hurricane Wings at Duxford, Middle Wallop and Wittering, and Hurricane Wings at Kenley, Northolt and North Weald. Before long, all would have re-equipped with the Spitfire.

But Armstrong knew that the War would not be won by fighter sweeps over the continent, or by bombing attacks that as yet were little more than pinpricks. The War would be won – or lost – by the battle that was developing with ever greater ferocity out there on the high seas.

After some further discussion, Van Berg drove Armstrong and Baird to an hotel in Eastchurch for lunch, as the messing facilities on the aerodrome were still under repair. On their return, as Armstrong and Baird walked out to the Harvard, Baird glanced up at the mid-afternoon sky, which was clear and at variance with the weather forecast, which had predicted low cloud and rain later in the day.

"We shan't be needing our overnight bags after all," he commented. "Looks like being a pleasant trip back to Crosby."

Armstrong looked sideways at him and grinned. "As a matter of fact, Dickie, we aren't going back to Crosby – not just yet, anyway," he told the surprised naval officer. "You know that I always like to see things for myself, and that's just what I intend to do. You and I are going to pay a little visit to Brest, courtesy of Bomber Command."

Chapter Five

Royal Air Force Station Oakington, Cambridge –
4 April 1941

"All I can say," Baird said with feeling, "is I'm glad we weren't here in January."

Armstrong made no response; the previous evening, in the bar of the Officers' Mess, they had been entertained by horror stories about the miseries endured by the Oakington personnel in the early weeks of the year, when the surface of the aerodrome had been either a morass of mud or a freezing, slippery ice sheet. Conditions had been so bad for a time that airmen working out in the open had been issued with a daily rum ration.

Oakington, six miles north-west of Cambridge, was a new airfield, completed at the end of 1940. It was now home to the massive Short Stirling bombers of No. 7 Squadron, which were only just getting into the swing of operations after suffering from a spate of minor but frustrating technical troubles. But it was not the Stirlings that interested the two visitors, who were standing on the balcony of the control tower, occasionally throwing a glance towards the northern sky. It was eleven o'clock in the morning.

Fortress England

Baird suddenly nudged his companion, and pointed. "There they are," he said. It took Armstrong a second or two to pick out what the Scot, who had phenomenal eyesight, was indicating: then he too made out half a dozen black specks, flying in two flights of three and growing rapidly larger. A few minutes later the specks had resolved themselves into four-engined bombers with deep fuselages and twin tail fins, readily identifiable as Handley Page Halifaxes. They were flying into Oakington, their forward operating base, from their usual airfield in North Yorkshire.

As yet there was only one Halifax squadron in RAF Bomber Command, and half of it was now bearing down on Oakington. Armstrong, with access to much secret and privileged information, had known that a raid on the enemy warships at Brest by the new heavy bombers had been planned for some time, and he had been in regular touch with the Halifax squadron commander, who knew as much as he needed to know about Armstrong's special duties squadron.

The officer who commanded the Halifax squadron was a New Zealander, a certain Wing Commander David Pittaway. In October 1939, while they were acting as liaison officers with Bomber Command, Armstrong and Baird had accompanied Pittaway – then a flight lieutenant – on a hazardous daylight bombing mission to the German naval base at Wilhelmshaven, a sortie that had cost the squadron nine Wellingtons out of twelve. Armstrong and Pittaway had both been injured after their Wellington crash-landed back at base afterwards; Baird had been rescued by a Dutch trawler after the aircraft in which he was flying was shot down into the North Sea.

Their paths had crossed again in June 1940 when Armstrong, attached to the French Air Force, had been flying from an airfield near the Alps in the last days before France's collapse. Pittaway's Wellingtons had landed there to refuel before setting out to bomb Genoa, and Armstrong had gone along for the ride. Once again, they had barely escaped with their lives after being shot down in error by a French night-fighter pilot, who had mistaken their Wellington for an intruding Italian bomber.

It all seemed a very long time ago.

The Halifaxes came in to land one by one, the throaty roar of their Rolls-Royce Merlin engines dwindling. Each aircraft reached its assigned dispersal point and trucks went out to pick up the crews. Armstrong and Baird made their way back to the Officers' Mess, knowing that the commissioned members of the Halifax crews would be dropped off there before the rest went on to the Sergeants' Mess.

They met Pittaway in the Mess ante-room, shortly before lunch. "You made it, then," the New Zealander said simply. Armstrong grinned at him as he shook his hand.

"Getting to be a habit," he replied. "You remember Dickie Baird, our intrepid naval aviator?"

"I do indeed," Pittaway said, greeting the Fleet Air Arm officer. "So this bloke has roped you into his private air force, then." It was a statement, not a question.

"My second in command," Armstrong told him. Pittaway nodded and beckoned to one of the dozen or so officers who were assembling in the ante-room, a flight lieutenant with a balding head and a substantial moustache. The New Zealander introduced him as Don Barker.

"You can fly with Don," he said to Baird. "He's safe enough. Been around for a while." Later, Baird discovered that Barker had flown Blenheims in the disastrous days of the Battle of France, and that he was one of the few survivors of the squadron to which he had then belonged.

The Mess dining room was practically deserted. Armstrong knew that the Stirling squadron resident at Oakington had been out on operations the night before – he had watched the aircraft taking off – and that it had been a long trip, so most of the aircrews were probably still in bed. The conversation over lunch was desultory, but that was usual with a mission in the offing. He guessed that Pittaway's crews, for security reasons, would not yet know the nature of tonight's target. That would be revealed at the briefing, which was to be held in a couple of hours' time. The ground crews would already be at work on the aircraft, checking all the systems – despite the fact that they would have been checked before the Halifaxes flew down to Oakington – and loading the bombs.

The Stirling crews were just starting to trickle into the dining room as Armstrong and the others were leaving. The visitors attracted one or two curious looks, but no one said anything. A few minutes later, over coffee, Armstrong quietly asked Pittaway what he thought of the Halifax. The New Zealander shrugged.

"It's early days yet," he admitted. "She has a good bomb

load – thirteen thousand pounds maximum – and she's got a range of eighteen hundred miles or so. She'll improve after Handley Page have carried out a few modifications. For instance, our Mark Ones don't have a mid-upper gun turret, but that's being fitted to the next batch, so I understand, and the power-operated nose gun turret is being dispensed with. It's too heavy, and causes too much drag. But the Halifax is streets ahead of the Stirling, which is a complete bloody heap. Its wings are too short, and it won't go above fourteen thousand feet with anything like a respectable bomb load."

Armstrong nodded. He was familiar with the sad tale of the Short Stirling: the bomber was originally to have had a wing span of 112 feet, which would have given it a good high altitude performance, but on the orders of the Air Ministry this had been reduced to ninety-nine feet so that the aircraft would fit into existing hangars. Its lack of an adequate operational ceiling made it very vulnerable to anti-aircraft fire.

The Halifax crews assembled in Oakington's briefing room at three o'clock. There were forty-two men in all, for each bomber carried a crew of seven. Armstrong and Baird sat at the back, the former reflecting that every briefing room in Bomber Command looked exactly the same, from the raised dais with its blackboard and maps – the latter set up by the Intelligence Officer, who was also present, and for the moment concealed by a curtain – to the aircraft recognition posters pinned to the walls.

Pittaway ascended the dais and stood facing the expectant crews for a moment, then turned and pulled a cord, drawing back the curtains to reveal a map of the English Channel area. A red ribbon stretched across it, from Oakington to Brest. In the audience, somebody groaned.

"All right, all right," Pittaway said, "so you'd rather be going to Berlin. Well, instead, you're going to Brest, together with one hundred and ten other aircraft – Wellingtons, Whitleys and Blenheims. As you will doubtless have guessed, your targets are the German warships there. And you'll be going in first."

There were more groans, and a flight sergeant with 'Canada' flashes on the shoulders of his tunic raised his hand.

"Excuse me, sir," he said politely, "but you keep using this little word 'you'. I take it you'll be coming along as well?"

Pittaway grinned at him as a few chuckles broke out. "Don't worry, Jacko. I want to see if your bombing's going to be any improvement on your last performance. Now then, back to business. We'll be going in at eight thousand feet to improve our chances of sighting the ships. With any luck, we'll be over Brest before the enemy has time to put up a smoke screen. We'll each be carrying four two thousand pounders, plus incendiaries and parachute flares. As well as hitting the ships, the idea is to light up the target like a Christmas tree, so that even if it's obscured by the time the main force arrives – and it won't be far behind us – it will be able to use our flares as an aiming point.

"Now, this isn't a long trip – three hundred nautical

miles to the target, or thereabouts – and it's over water all the way after we cross the English coast, so we don't have to worry about fighters or flak until we are on the run-up to Brest, across this little peninsula here." He picked up a snooker cue which had been propped against the wall and tapped the map with it.

"The biggest danger," he went on, "will be getting tangled up with aircraft of the main force, some of which we shall actually overtake en route, so watch out for that. They'll be at a higher level than us, in theory, but you never know. That's all I have to say for the moment, so I'm going to hand you over to the 'Spy', who will want to give you the good news about flak defences and so on."

The Intelligence Officer, an immaculately uniformed individual with the single blue ring of a flying officer around the sleeves of his tunic – from one cuff of which a spotted handkerchief protruded – adjusted his glasses and took Pittaway's place on the dais. He addressed the assembly in a measured, cultured voice. Armstrong had met him in the Mess the previous evening, and had learned that the Intelligence Officer had, in a previous existence, been a senior curator in a famous museum. This war, he mused, was certainly doing strange things to people.

"Gentlemen," the Intelligence Officer said, "I know that to many of you, attacks on the German Navy must seem like a waste of effort. It must seem that you would be far better employed in attacking Germany's war industries. But let me assure you that the kind of operation you will be flying tonight is more vital than any other to the survival of Britain.

"Unlike the Royal Navy, which is divided between the Atlantic and the Mediterranean, the Germans can afford to concentrate all their naval assets in the Atlantic. Their submarine fleet is increasing all the time, but at the moment their fast, heavily-armed warships constitute the main threat to our convoys. The position, according to our latest intelligence reports, is that three of their heavy cruisers, the *Scheer, Lutzow* and *Hipper,* are in Kiel; another, the *Prinz Eugen,* is at Gdynia on the Baltic, along with a new battleship, the *Bismarck.* Another battleship, the *Tirpitz,* is fitting out at Wilhelmshaven. Our photo-recce boys are keeping a close watch on all these vessels, and if any of them try to break out into the Atlantic, we ought to know about it in good time. Besides, Bomber Command is making constant attacks on Kiel, and although results haven't been very promising so far, there's always the chance that our bombers might inflict damage on the cruisers and put one or more of them out of action."

Armstrong and Baird exchanged glances. Kiel, they knew, was a difficult target, and heavily defended; although the town had been hit, there was no evidence that the warships had suffered at all.

The Intelligence Officer turned to the map and pointed at Brest.

"Here, then, is the main threat," he said. "The *Scharnhorst* and *Gneisenau.* At any moment, they might venture out into the Atlantic again to prey on our convoys. But we think they are waiting for something. There are indications that some – perhaps even all of – the heavy warships might try to break out from their locations in northern Germany and sail for the French ports. If that happens, the Germans will have a concentration of firepower the Royal Navy will be hard pressed to match. So the sinking of those two battlecruisers is of paramount importance. In fact, it's a matter of survival."

He paused to let his words sink in, then continued with his part of the briefing, pointing out the sites of the main anti-aircraft batteries protecting Brest harbour. Including the warships' weapons, the bombers would have to run the gauntlet of some 250 guns in and around the anchorage.

The Meteorological Officer, next on the dais, predicted rain squalls en route to the target, but clear skies over it. There would be no moon; it was in its last quarter, and would already have set two hours before take-off time, which was fixed for 2100.

Later, as Armstrong and Baird made their way back to the Officers' Mess, Baird glanced at his watch and made what, to his companion, seemed a strange remark.

"I ought to be coming out of church about now," he said quietly.

Puzzled, Armstrong looked at him. "What?"

"It's Good Friday," Baird said, "and I'm a Catholic, albeit not a very good one. Catholics celebrate Mass at three o'clock on Good Friday afternoon. My folks will have been doing just that right now, in the little church in Stornoway."

"Good Lord! I hadn't realised that it was Easter weekend," Armstrong admitted. "I should have done, when fish was the only thing on the lunchtime menu. Anyway, there'll be a Roman Catholic chapel somewhere

58

on the station. Can't you go later on? There's plenty of time."

Baird nodded, and they walked on in silence. Armstrong had never given much thought to religion; his parents, although professing to be Church of England, did not attend services, with the exception perhaps of Harvest Festival, and he had a sneaking suspicion that many of those who went to church regularly did so as a matter of social ritual, rather than genuine belief. Still, he thought, each to his own.

Back at the Mess, Armstrong did what he always did when there was time to kill before an operational sortie: he went to bed. Sleep never eluded him on such occasions, and it was the best way he knew of cutting out the irksome waiting period. Later, after being awakened by one of the Mess stewards, he showered and shaved; that was another ritual, based on the theory that if he should be shot down over enemy territory and survive, it would be a good thing to enter captivity clean and shaven.

He joined the others for the meal. Afterwards, there was a short wait until the trucks came to pick them up, having already collected the NCO aircrew. At bomber bases all over eastern England a similar ritual was being enacted as the hundred or so crews assigned to tonight's operation headed for their bombers. The Whitleys, based in Yorkshire and a good thirty miles per hour slower than the other bombers that made up the attacking force, would already have taken off.

To Armstrong, used to nothing larger than twin-engined

Blenheims and Beaufighters, the Halifax appeared awesomely large as he settled himself into the small spare seat that swung out from the starboard side of the cockpit and glanced down through the side window at the ground, twenty feet below. With all the crew in their positions, Pittaway ran through the lengthy pre-flight checklist. The engines had already been primed by the ground crew; now, one by one, they burst into life with the harsh crackling, spitting sound that was peculiar to the Rolls-Royce Merlin. When all four were running smoothly, Pittaway stuck his arm through his side window, waving to the ground crew to remove the chocks. The airmen pulled the chocks clear of the main wheels and, in the dim light of the dispersal, gave a thumbs-up signal to indicate that their job was done.

Pittaway released the brakes in a hiss of compressed air and the Halifax moved slowly forward out of its dispersal, rumbling along the taxi track, followed by the other five bombers. At the entrance to the runway he ran up the engines to full power in turn, each time checking the two-stage blower, propeller pitch control and the magnetos. Satisfied that all was well, he started his take-off checks.

"Okay. Ready for take-off, wireless op."

Behind the two pilots, the wireless operator, who had taken up temporary station in the perspex astrodome on top of the fuselage, flashed a light towards the control tower, for strict radio silence was being observed. A green light answered and the signaller scrambled back into his position in the nose, below the pilot's seat. The Halifax's nose was nine feet deep, allowing plenty of room for the pilot, wireless operator, navigator – whose plotting table was under the front gun turret – and the gunner. The flight engineer's console was immediately to the rear of the flight deck.

Pittaway turned the Halifax on to the runway. Armstrong listened over the intercom as the pilot went through the checklist.

"Flaps thirty . . . radiators closed . . . throttles locked. Prepare to take off. All clear behind, rear gunner?"

"All clear behind, skipper."

Pittaway placed his hand on the four throttles, mounted close together on their quadrant in the centre of the instrument panel, and eased them forward.

"Full power." The New Zealander opened the throttles wide and the Halifax accelerated forward with a terrific surge of power as Pittaway released the brakes, which he had applied while the engines were being run up. The tail rose and the lights of the runway flarepath flickered past the bomber's wingtips as it gathered speed, rumbling and vibrating.

At length the rumbling and the vibration ceased. The Halifax was airborne.

"Climbing power . . . wheels up . . . flaps up."

They climbed steadily into the night sky, turning gently on to a south-easterly heading, and levelled off at 8,000 feet, throttling back to cruising power. The airspeed indicator showed 220 miles per hour. They flew on over a darkened southern England, passing to the east of London, their track taking them over Reading and across the coast at Bournemouth. Ahead lay the broad expanse of the English Channel, dark and sinister.

They had been flying for about fifty minutes when a sudden jolt rocked the aircraft. Pittaway immediately altered course to starboard and the buffeting ceased.

"Something's slipstream," Pittaway remarked. "One of the Whitleys, I guess. He's lower than he ought to be." They saw nothing and flew on. From time to time, the navigator issued small course corrections. At length, he announced that Guernsey was twenty-five miles off the bomber's port wing, and that they would be making landfall on the enemy coast in thirty minutes. The six Halifaxes were now in the vanguard of the bomber stream.

After a few more minutes, the navigator left his plotting table and crawled forward into the nose, lying prone on his bomb-aiming position mattress. He plugged himself into the intercom socket there and checked that the pilot could hear him. There was silence for a while, and then:

"Enemy coast ahead, skipper. Spot on. Whoops – there go the searchlights."

Artmstrong, peering ahead through the perspex, suddenly found himself dazzled as half a dozen searchlight beams, still some distance away, speared up into the night. A few more minutes crept by, and then the navigator/bomb aimer announced that they were crossing the coast, right on track, with twenty miles to run to their target.

"Okay," Pittaway said. "Keep your eyes peeled, gunners. There may be night fighters. Hang on to your seat, Ken. This could be rough." It was an unneccessary order; Armstrong was already hanging on to his seat, and feeling extremely vulnerable. The probing searchlights had still not found them.

"This is beautiful," the navigator said. "I can see everything." Although there was no moon, the harbour area ahead of them was clearly defined against the surrounding land.

"Bomb doors open."

The Halifax shuddered slightly as Pittaway pulled a lever and the bomb-bay doors swung down into the slipstream. The four 2,000-pound bombs the aircraft was carrying swayed gently in their shackles.

"Left two degrees, skipper. I can see the dock area nicely . . . that's good. That's good. Hold her steady."

The flak started to come up, wicked red flashes bursting across the sky above them. The German gunners were misjudging their height badly. Armstrong prayed that they would keep on doing so. Although mainly a fighter and photo-recce pilot, he had flown on several bombing missions, and had found every one more nerve-racking than the one before. This, he decided, was not for him.

In the nose, the navigator-turned-bomb aimer was keeping up his chant, exhorting the pilot to hold the aircraft steady. Suddenly, there was a bright orange flash, dead ahead, and a pungent reek of explosive invaded the cockpit. Pittaway fought hard to keep on course as the blast wave struck the aircraft.

"That was close. Everybody okay?" The front gunner answered, in a rather shaken voice, that he was. The navigator went on with his unruffled monologue as though nothing had happened.

"Steady, steady, steady . . . right a touch . . . okay, steady . . . Bombs away!"

The Halifax leaped as its three and a half tons of bombs dropped away. The flak was coming up thick and fast now, the shell bursts of the large calibre weapons intermingled with glowing dots that were the shells of quick-firing automatic weapons. The whole effect was like a storm of orange and red sleet, rising unnaturally from the ground.

"Bomb doors closed. Let's get out of it!"

The Halifax thundered over the harbour, pursued by the anti-aircraft fire. Armstrong resisted a strong urge to close his eyes.

Then the rear gunner piped up over the intercom, "There go the flashes, skipper . . . I counted three. No sign of number four. That's all. Looks as though they're in the docks area, though. There's a glow − I think we started a fire."

He sounded disappointed, as though he had been expecting a massive explosion.

Pittaway grunted and continued on course, taking the Halifax some way out to sea before asking the navigator, now back at his table, for a course for home. As the bomber swung round on a north-easterly heading, Armstrong saw more flashes light up the sky over Brest as the other Halifaxes unloaded their bombs. He continued to watch for a long time, craning his neck, until the glow receded over the horizon.

As the last of the attacking bombers droned away, Brest was the scene of feverish activity. Neither of the warships had been damaged in the attack, but one bomb had hit the Continental Hotel, killing several German naval officers who were staying there. But it was a

second bomb that was to produce unforeseen consequences.

The *Scharnhorst*, having been overhauled in dry dock,
was now back in the harbour and moored to the north quay,
protected by a torpedo boom. The *Gneisenau*, however,
was still in dry dock, and a bomb fell close to her.
It failed to explode, and because of the danger it was
decided to move the battlecruiser out of the dock while
the missile was rendered harmless. There was no room
at the quay for the *Gneisenau*, so she would have to be
run out into the harbour until the bomb was defused. The
risk was judged to be acceptable. After all, the operation
should not take more than a few hours.

In the following dawn, as Armstrong and the others –
all of whom had returned safely – slept off their post-flight
meal of bacon and eggs, a blue-painted Spitfire of the
photo-reconnaissance unit based at Oakington took off and
climbed to 28,000 feet, heading for Brest. The photographs
she would bring back would be among the most important
of the War.

Chapter Six

"Familiar territory for you, this, Dickie," Armstrong said over the intercom, as he brought the Harvard in to land. Baird gave a grunt in reply; he had spent some time as officer commanding the target-towing flight at another Cornish airfield, St Merryn, and had not enjoyed the experience. Armstrong had rescued him from that, when his own special duties squadron was in the process of formation.

Armstrong touched down on one of the airfield's runways – their construction had been completed just a few weeks earlier – and taxied up to the Watch Office, where he and Baird were met by the Commanding Officer of a Beaufort squadron on temporary detachment to St Eval from its usual base at North Coates. He was also a wing commander, and was far from pleased when Armstrong told him what his squadron's target was to be.

"The *Gneisenau*. In the middle of Brest harbour? Bloody suicide! We wouldn't have more than one chance in a thousand of getting through. Brest is one of the most

66

heavily-defended targets in Europe. What hope of success d'you think a torpedo attack would stand?"

The wing commander had already been alerted by Headquarters Coastal Command that his crews were to stand by for a mission of the utmost importance, and that they would be briefed by Armstrong. The latter sympathised with him, but was prepared to argue the case firmly. He carried with him the package of photographs developed from the film brought back by the PRU Spitfire earlier in the day, and when the wing commander examined them in the security of his office a while later, what he saw did nothing to lessen his sense of foreboding.

The inner harbour of Brest was protected by a stone mole bending around it from the west, and at its furthest point the mole was less than a mile from the quayside. The *Gneisenau* was anchored at right angles to the quay, some 500 yards from the eastern boundary of the harbour, about midway between mole and quay.

"Look," the wing commander said, indicating the photographs spread out on his desk top. "Put yourself in the position of an attacking pilot. In order to aim your torpedo, your aircraft would have to traverse the outer harbour and approach the mole at an angle to the anchored ship, which means that it would be exposed to crossfire from the gun batteries which we know are positioned on these two arms of land that encircle the outer harbour. And there's more. See these ships in the outer harbour, just outside the mole? They're flak ships, guarding the approach to the battlecruiser. And there are batteries of guns on this rising ground here, behind the quay, with even more around the inner harbour. Oh, and don't forget the *Scharnhorst* and *Gneisenau*. Even if the other guns didn't get you by some miracle, theirs certainly would. I don't like the expression 'wall of steel', but that's exactly what it amounts to."

Dickie Baird, who had considerable experience of dropping torpedoes, chipped in.

"I have to say the wing commander is right, Ken. Look – even supposing an aircraft did get through, the pilot would have to line it up and aim and drop his torpedo before he actually crossed the mole, so that the tin fish would have the longest possible distance to run to its target. We've already said that the distance from the mole to the *Gneisenau* is no more than five hundred yards; if the torpedo were dropped within this range it wouldn't have time to arm itself and settle down to its running depth, which means that it would pass under the warship."

The wing commander nodded. "Yes. Everything depends on the pilot's approach to the mole being made at roughly the right dropping angle. He'd have only a few seconds between sighting the *Gneisenau* and dropping his torpedo, and there'd be no room for anything but the smallest adjustments to his course. During those few seconds, every gun in and around the anchorage would be firing at him. Talk about the charge of the Light Brigade . . . and what about after the drop? He might escape the fire of the bigger guns if he could stay down on the deck, but the instant he made his drop he would have to pull up to avoid the rising ground, so he'd be silhouetted against the sky like a clay pigeon. I'm telling you, it would be sheer suicide."

He shook his head and sighed, as though in surrender, then looked directly at Armstrong.

"All right. I know the problems. We're the only torpedo-bomber squadron within striking distance of Brest; the rest are scattered all over the shop. The trouble is, I've only got six aircraft. The other three are out on a strike. The best I can do is get the remaining six away at dawn. The *Gneisenau* is certain to be protected by torpedo nets, so I propose to send three aircraft in with bombs to rupture the nets. They'll have an element of surprise, so they might just get away with it. I'll send off the torpedo-carriers first, so that they'll be loitering just off the harbour when the bombers go in. After that, it'll be up to God and Providence. Let's get the crews together, and get on with it."

The briefing did not take long. After a meal, Armstrong and Baird found themselves a couple of beds and snatched a few hours' rest before emerging to watch the Beauforts taking off into the pre-dawn darkness. It had been raining heavily and the aerodrome was badly waterlogged; the three torpedo-carrying Beauforts got away all right, but two of the bomb-carriers became hopelessly bogged down and only one followed the first three into the dawn. It was now 0515, and sunrise was a quarter of an hour away over the eastern horizon.

The crew of the bomb-carrying Beaufort, forging on over the Channel through mist and rain, became lost. When daylight came and they managed to pinpoint their position, they found that they were many miles to the south of Brest. They dropped their bombs on an enemy convoy that was making its way along the coast and headed for home.

Meanwhile, two of the torpedo-carrying Beauforts had arrived off Brest independently. The first to do so was piloted by Flying Officer Ken Campbell, a twenty-four-year-old Scot from Ayrshire who had joined the RAF just after the outbreak of war. The second, arriving a few minutes later, was flown by an Australian, Flying Officer Jimmy Hyde. The squadron's most experienced pilot, Hyde had been awarded the Distinguished Flying Cross only a few days earlier.

In accordance with their orders, Hyde and Campbell loitered outside the harbour, awaiting the arrival of the bomb-carrying Beauforts. Their instructions were to make their torpedo attack only when they saw the explosions of the bombs. They had no means of knowing that two of the Beauforts had not even managed to take off, and that the other had got lost. And there was no sign, so far, of the third torpedo Beaufort.

Both aircraft continued to fly in broad circles, skimming through banks of mist and low cloud that hid the harbour area. They had been the first to take off, at 0430, and it was becoming daylight. Hyde knew that if they delayed their attack for much longer, their chances of survival would be infinitesimal. Yet there was no sign of the bombers, and Hyde knew that if they did not arrive soon, the attack would have to be aborted.

Suddenly, Hyde caught a glimpse of a Beaufort flashing past, just underneath him. It had the code-letter 'X' on its fuselage, and he knew that it was Campbell's aircraft.

Moreover, it was heading straight for the mist-shrouded harbour. Hyde wondered what the other pilot was up to; there had still been no bomb explosions. He went on circling, determined not to sacrifice the lives of his crew needlessly. There would be little point, he reasoned, in getting themselves shot down and killed only to have their tin fish stopped short of the battlecruiser by a torpedo net.

Campbell, meanwhile, raced across the outer harbour at 300 feet, heading for the right-hand end of the mole, his Beaufort slipping in and out of the low-lying cloud. Ahead of him, grey blurs in the murk, he could just see the flak ships; their gun crews, and those in the emplacements around the harbour, were desperately searching for the speeding torpedo bomber, which they could hear but not yet see.

Campbell put his aircraft into a shallow dive towards the east end of the mole. Beyond it, he could see a huge dark bulk that was the stern of the *Gneisenau*. He turned to starboard and swung back to port, making an angle of forty-five degrees with the battleship. He sped between the two flak ships at fifty feet above the water; they still did not open fire, although by now the Beaufort must have been clearly visible.

The mole was 200 yards ahead of the racing aircraft. As it loomed up in front of the Beaufort he lifted the nose a little to clear it, levelled out again and released the torpedo. It seemed to hang under the Beaufort for several seconds as the two flashed across the mole, then its nose dipped towards the water.

71

At last, as the Beaufort pulled up to the left towards the sheltering clouds, the guns opened up, filling the sky with a rain of 37-mm and 20-mm shells. Glowing balls of fire seemed to pass through the Beaufort; it faltered in its climb, turned over on its back and plunged into the harbour in a glare of exploding fuel tanks, shedding debris. Neither Campbell nor the other members of his crew – the navigator, Sergeant James Scott, a Canadian from Toronto, the wireless operator, Sergeant Mulliss, a Somerset farmer before the War and the rear gunner, Sergeant Hillman, a Londoner who had once been chauffeur to a doctor's family in Barnsley, Yorkshire – had stood a chance of getting out.

The torpedo ran on across the harbour. It struck the *Gneisenau* aft and its 500-pound warhead exploded below the waterline, blasting a great hole in the ship. Immediately, she began to take on tons of water.

Thirty minutes later, as the Germans launched almost every vessel in the harbour to support the badly damaged battlecruiser and damage control crews laboured to pump out the water, the third torpedo-carrying Beaufort arrived off Brest. Its pilot, Sergeant Camp, had gone a long way off course in atrocious weather. Now, as Campbell had done, he prepared to make a lone attack.

At sea level, Camp flew between the two arms of land that encircled the outer harbour. Ahead of him he could see nothing – the mist, combined with the smoke of earlier shellbursts, was too thick. Suddenly, the sky around his Beaufort erupted in a red and orange glare as the anti-aircraft gunners targeted it. Unable to see a thing, with no real idea of the course he must follow to locate the *Gneisenau*, he prudently pulled away in a climbing turn to the east and found himself in cloud cover almost at once.

The next day, a photo-reconnaissance Spitfire came back with evidence that the *Gneisenau* was once again in dry dock. But the photographs could not reveal the extent of the damage Campbell's torpedo had inflicted on the mighty warship: her injuries were to keep her under repair for eight crucial months. And when the authorities in London eventually learned the full story, Flying Officer Kenneth Campbell was awarded a posthumous Victoria Cross.

So the first blow had been struck in the battle to thwart the German Navy's plans to send out a powerful battle squadron into the North Atlantic. But good news is often tempered with bad. Even as Ken Campbell was carrying out the last gallant, despairing action of his young life, German forces were smashing their way into Yugoslavia as a preliminary to the invasion and occupation of Greece.

They struck with twenty-seven divisions, seven of them armoured, the whole force supported by 1,200 aircraft. The three fighter squadrons of the RAF in Greece, equipped with a mixture of Gloster Gladiator biplanes and more modern Hawker Hurricanes, had enjoyed considerable success against the Italians, claiming ninety-three enemy aircraft destroyed in the first three months of 1941 for the loss of only ten of their own; but now they faced a different and much more formidable foe.

Even so, early skirmishing between the RAF and the *Luftwaffe* produced encouraging results; over Eastern

Macedonia, where the RAF was providing air cover for Greek ground forces, twelve Hurricanes of No. 33 Squadron encountered twenty Me 109s and claimed five of them for no loss. Such good fortune, however, was not to last. Following a spell of atrocious weather, which severely limited air operations for the best part of a week, the German forces – after seizing their principal objectives in Yugoslavia – launched an all-out offensive against Greece with overwhelming air support.

The RAF fighters – now strengthened by the addition of a fourth squadron hurriedly deployed to Greece from North Africa – were committed to patrolling over the Allied positions and to escorting Blenheims attacking the enemy by daylight. On 14 April, the Hurricanes were heavily in action against Junkers 87 *Stukas* that were subjecting the Australia and New Zealand Army Corps to furious dive-bombing attacks in the Thermopylae area; the British fighters claimed some successes and the *Luftwaffe* retaliated by striking hard in a series of low-level attacks on the RAF airfields. At Larissa, on the morning of 15 April, twenty Me 109s pounced just as three of No. 33 Squadron's Hurricanes were taking off. Two were shot down and their pilots killed, but not before one of them had accounted for a 109; the third Hurricane pilot, a young and inexperienced sergeant, not only escaped the onslaught but succeeded in destroying a second 109, afterwards landing back at Larissa without a bullet hole in his aircraft.

By 17 April, it was becoming clear that the Allied front in Greece was rapidly collapsing, and Air Vice-Marshal D'Albiac – commanding the RAF contingent – ordered the withdrawal of the Hurricane squadrons to the Athens area to provide air cover for an evacuation that was becoming increasingly likely. The withdrawal was carried out under constant pressure from the *Luftwaffe*, but the hard-pressed RAF fighters continued to give more punishment than they took. No. 208 Squadron, the last to withdraw, had a narrow escape: just after the Hurricanes had taken off from Paramythia, which was still littered with the wreckage of forty-odd Yugoslav aircraft destroyed in an earlier attack, the *Luftwaffe* once again appeared in strength and wiped out a Greek Gladiator squadron on the ground.

By 19 April, the four Hurricane squadrons in Greece could muster no more than twenty-two serviceable aircraft, dispersed on the airfields of Menidi and Eleusis. These airfields, in fact, were large enough to have accommodated five squadrons of Hurricanes, but there were simply not enough Hurricanes in the Middle East to provide replacement aircraft for the embattled units already in Greece, let alone bring five squadrons up to strength.

The depleted squadrons had barely arrived at their new locations when they were compelled to fight a series of savage actions against large formations of enemy bombers and fighters attacking Piraeus harbour and the airfields near Athens. The climax of these battles came on 20 April, when fifteen Hurricanes of Nos. 33 and 80 Squadrons, all that could be mustered, took off again and again to intercept the Germans. There were many deeds of heroism among the dwindling band of Hurricane pilots that day; to give just one example, the Hurricane flown by Flying Officer Harry Starrett was hit and set on fire, and instead of baling out Starrett – knowing how desperately Hurricanes were needed – flew the aircraft back to base and made a wheels-up landing. As the Hurricane slid to a stop the glycol tank exploded, and although Starrett managed to stagger clear of the wreck his burns were so severe that he died two days later.

The battles of 19–20 April cost the RAF five more Hurricanes, and on the 21st, with the danger that the German *Panzer* divisions might reach Athens before the British forces could withdraw to the beachhead, the British C-in-C, General Sir Henry Maitland Wilson, ordered the evacuation to begin immediately. On the following day the handful of surviving Hurricanes were flown to Argos, a small Greek training airfield, from where they were expected to cover the evacuation. Together with reinforcement aircraft flown in from Crete, this rearguard fighter force numbered just twenty-one aircraft.

By nightfall on 23 April, the Hurricane force had virtually ceased to exist. In a series of strafing attacks that lasted nearly three-quarters of an hour, more than thirty Me 110s pounced on Argos airfield and destroyed thirteen Hurricanes on the ground. At first light the next day, the last seven aircraft were ordered to fly to Crete.

It was the end. What was to become known as the Greek fiasco had cost the Royal Air Force 209 aircraft of all types – 72 in combat, 55 in attacks on the ground and 82 destroyed or abandoned during the evacuation because there was no fuel to fly them out or because their airfields were too heavily cratered.

Over 50,000 men were brought out of Greece and

evacuated to Crete and Egypt by a fleet of vessels – 32 warships, mostly destroyers, 19 transports and many smaller craft. Two destroyers and four transports were sunk by enemy aircraft.

Greece and the comparatively calm waters of the eastern Mediterranean were a long way from the stormy seas of the North Atlantic, but when he learned of the German invasion on 7 April, Armstrong knew full well what it would mean. The Royal Navy would now be compelled to divert more warships from the Atlantic arena in order to retain superiority in the Mediterranean, which would mean fewer escorts for the Atlantic convoys. The Germans must surely choose this moment to make an all-out onslaught on the merchant fleet. It was an opportunity they could not afford to pass over.

Chapter Seven

Armstrong had been back at Crosby-on-Eden less than a week when an urgent telephone call caused him to pack his overnight bag again. The caller was Air Commodore John Glendenning, a staff officer at the Air Ministry to whom Armstrong was directly responsible for all operational matters.

"Have you flown a Hudson, Ken?" Glendenning wanted to know. Armstrong replied that he had. One of the Lockheed patrol bombers had been temporarily attached to the photographic reconnaisance unit in which he served earlier, and he had taken the opportunity to have himself checked out on it.

"Good. In that case, I've a job for you. A very important job. Report to Tangmere the day after tomorrow. You'll be briefed at ten a.m. Oh, and bring that French-speaking flight commander of yours along. The Polish chap, what's-his-name."

So it was that Armstrong, greatly mystified and accompanied by Kalinski, the latter's sniffles now cured, flew down to RAF Tangmere, near Chichester on the Sussex coast, on the morning of Saturday the thirteenth of April – not a good day to embark on anything perilous, Armstrong thought, but at least it wasn't a Friday.

As soon as the Harvard had rolled to a stop its two occupants were spirited away by armed RAF police, not to the briefing room, as Armstrong had anticipated, but to a picturesque cottage opposite the aerodrome's main gate. Glendenning was waiting for them, and as the policemen made themselves scarce he showed the newcomers into a comfortable parlour furnished with armchairs, a table and a sofa. Covering the whole of one wall there was a map of France and the Low Countries. A tea urn stood on the table, with some cups and a plate of biscuits nearby. They helped themselves gratefully.

"I'll come straight to the point," Glendenning told them as they drank. "I want you to fly to France, tonight, land there, drop off some people and fly back again. Simple, really."

Armstrong gaped at him, teacup poised halfway to his lips. The taciturn Kalinksi acted as though he hadn't heard.

The air commodore indicated the wall map. He found Rennes and moved his finger westwards until it stopped at a small blue patch a few miles north of Pontivy. "This is a reservoir," he explained. "Immediately to the north of it there is a flat expanse of ground. It's clear of obstacles and, so we are informed, firm enough to take a Hudson."

Armstrong wondered just who Glendenning's informants were, but made no comment.

"There'll be a reception committee waiting for you," the air commodore went on, "and they'll light a flarepath for you as soon as they hear your engines. You'll cross the enemy coast here, midway between Cherbourg and Le Havre; Bomber Command will be carrying out diversionary attacks on both places, so you'll be going in under cover of those. The plan is for you to fly due south until you are abeam Rennes, then turn west and approach the target area from inland. I'm afraid I can't tell you anything about your passengers, but it's vital that you deliver them safely. A lot depends on the job they have to do."

Armstrong could not help noticing that the landing ground was about forty miles from Brest, and guessed that the passengers' mission, whatever it was, must have something to do with the German warships there.

Glendenning did not enlighten him, but said, "Take-off is scheduled for twenty-two hundred. That will get you to the landing zone shortly after midnight GMT, well inside the hours of curfew imposed by the German occupation forces. All the maps you will need are in this, and also the weather forecast for tonight." He fished in a briefcase and pulled out a buff folder, which he laid on the table. "Your wireless operator will be joining you in half an hour; I suggest you get your flight plan sorted out, then spend a couple of hours this afternoon practising short landings and take-offs. The Hudson is in number two hangar. You won't be carrying a navigator – there isn't room. You'll have to manage the navigation between you."

"I'll be happy to stay at home," Kalinski said, and meant it. Glendenning looked at him unsmilingly. "We need you along because of your language ability," he told the Pole. "Your passengers have no more than a smattering of English. Besides which, you are a pilot; if anything should happen to Wing Commander Armstrong, you will be able to take over. Now, are there any questions?"

Armstrong had dozens, but he knew that he would not get answers to them. One aspect, though, was puzzling him.

"Wouldn't it be a lot easier to parachute these people into France, sir?" he asked. "A lot less risky, too, I should think."

Glendenning nodded. "It would, but it's out of the question. Your passengers will be carrying certain equipment with them, and it's too fragile to drop. Well, that's about all, except for me to wish you good luck. You'll be eating here; I'll arrange for transport to take you out to your aircraft later on."

The air commodore put on his gold-braided cap and departed without another word. They heard him start his car and drive off. Armstrong opened the folder and spread the maps out on the table top. Glendenning had thought of everything; he had also provided a navigational computer, the type that could be strapped to one's knee, a protractor, a ruler and some pencils.

They had almost completed their preliminary flight planning when there was a knock at the door and a man wearing the rank braid of a pilot officer entered the room, saluted Armstrong and introduced himself as Wilson, their wireless operator. They stared at him in amazement. For one thing, he wore no flying brevet; for another, he sported thick-lensed spectacles.

"I'm a specialist," he explained. "Not proper aircrew at

all. I've got certain tasks to carry out, you see. I do hope I shan't be in the way."

He spoke as though he were about to be setting out on a Sunday school outing, rather than an operation which might end in death for all of them or, even worse, in a Gestapo torture cell.

It turned out that Glendenning had thought of that eventuality, too. A little later, a medical officer arrived bearing a carton. He delved into it, produced a handful of small, transparent packages, each one marked with a different colour, and held them up in turn.

"Just in case things don't quite work out as planned," he remarked in what Armstrong thought was an unduly cheerful tone. "These are pills to resist fatigue, and these produce a high fever and every symptom of typhoid. If you should be taken prisoner, they could well get you out of a tight fix by persuading the Germans that you belong in a hospital rather than a prison cell, from which escape would obviously be a good deal more difficult. And finally, we have these."

He opened one of the little packages and a glass capsule rolled into his palm. He held it out so they could see it.

"Concentrated arsenic," he said mildly. "Inside the capsule it's quite harmless; you can keep it in your mouth and even swallow it. But break it between your teeth and you're dead in less than a minute – about forty-five seconds is the average for a normal, healthy person. It's not a pleasant way to go, but preferable to some of the alternatives, should you fall into enemy hands. Well, I think that's all. Do help yourselves to these." He counted out three sets of packages, laid them side by side in a neat row on the table, gave a beaming smile and went away.

"Well, that's cheered me up no end," Armstrong muttered, resolving to have nothing to do with that particular form of self-execution. Wilson, it seemed, felt the same, but Kalinski picked up his. Sensing the others looking at him, he said: "Oh, it's not for me. But if we do end up in the bag, it might come in handy for dropping into somebody's coffee."

They were forced to agree with him. Changing their minds, they picked up their little packages and put them in their pockets.

After they had eaten an excellent lunch of steak and chips, they were driven out to the Hudson by their police escort. The aircraft was parked outside a hangar that was set some distance apart from the rest; at first sight it looked like any other Coastal Command Hudson, with its dark grey upper surfaces and pale green belly, but then Armstrong saw that the gun turret had been removed, presumably to save weight and add to the aircraft's range. Canvas 'bucket' seats had been fitted to either side of the fuselage interior, and the wireless operator's table was crammed with equipment of a type neither Armstrong nor Kalinski recognised. Wilson hesitated by the table as Armstrong and Kalinski made their way forward towards the Hudson's glazed nose, then settled himself into his seat and began to make rapid notes on a pad.

As Armstrong taxied out to the take-off point a few minutes later, the radio specialist's voice sounded over the intercom.

"Sir, I wonder if you could alter the night-flying test a bit and take the aircraft up to twenty thousand feet over the coast? I'd like to check out some of my equipment, and it works best from that altitude."

Armstrong agreed with some reluctance, as he wanted to practice his short landing and take-off techniques, but he sensed that Wilson's job was an important one. The Hudson's twin Wright Cyclone radial engines roared healthily as it lifted away from the aerodrome and settled into a long climb, its pilot turning west over the Isle of Wight. Over the radio, Armstrong had made sure that the coastal defences were aware of his movements; this was a highly sensitive area, and people were understandably trigger-happy.

From 20,000 feet the view across the Channel was magnificent. Over Lyme Bay, Wilson asked Armstrong to fly a series of courses while he made some fine adjustments to his radio gear. It was quite comfortable in the Hudson's roomy cockpit, and from his position in the nose Kalinski kept up a running commentary, drawing the pilot's attention to shipping far below and to a pair of Spitfires, which appeared from nowhere and formated with the Hudson for a while before disappearing in the direction of Cornwall; but Armstrong, conscious of the dangerous and difficult mission ahead of him, was glad when Wilson announced that he had completed his checks.

Returning to Tangmere, he spent an hour on the aerodrome circuit, practicing take-offs and landings at various flap and power settings, approaching to land and climbing away at different angles until he found the optimum. At length, he decided to call it an afternoon and taxied in, shutting down the engines. The RAF police escorted the crew back to the cottage; there was nothing to do now but wait. Wilson appeared tense and tried to immerse himself in a book, feeling envious of Armstrong and Kalinski, who settled down in comfortable armchairs and promptly fell asleep.

"Coffee and sandwiches, sir?"

Armstrong came awake with a start to find an airman standing by his chair, bearing a tray laden with food. He sat up, rubbing his eyes. The clock on the mantelpiece told him that he had been asleep for four hours. He glared reproachfully at Kalinski, who grinned at him through a mouthful of corned beef and bread. 'Bully beef', rather surprisingly, had become one of the Pole's favourite foods.

"You shouldn't have let me sleep for so long," Armstrong said. Kalinski merely shrugged.

"You looked as though you could do with it," was all he said.

Armstrong had to agree with him. The short sleep had done him a lot of good, and he felt substantially refreshed. He took himself off to the bathroom, washed away any remaining tiredness, then returned to attack the coffee and sandwiches.

Afterwards, he and Kalinski made a final check of their flight plan. Armstrong had no worries about finding their objective – he knew that Kalinski was an expert navigator, as well as a highly skilled pilot, and for the outward leg of the flight they would have the benefit of a waning moon, which would set shortly before midnight.

Armstrong glanced at the clock: it was 2115. He wondered where their passengers were, and presumed that they would be taken straight out to the aircraft.

"All right," he said finally, "let's get kitted out. It'll soon be time to get the Hudson wound up. Don't forget your flight rations."

The latter had been made up for them. Some paper bags on the table contained more sandwiches, a couple of cold sausages wrapped in greaseproof paper, chocolate, barley sugar and chewing gum. Although it seemed unappetising now, it would all be eaten on the return flight, for their appetites then would be sharpened by adrenalin.

A few minutes later, their police escort arrived to ferry them out to the aircraft. As they alighted from the vehicle, they noticed a small group of people, huddled beside the Hudson's fuselage to derive some small shelter from the stiff and chilly wind. Kalinski spoke in French to a man who was apparently their leader, then ushered them aboard the aircraft and showed them how to strap themselves into their uncomfortable seats. Wilson was already fiddling with his radio equipment and Armstrong was in the cockpit, waiting to start up. Kalinski settled himself into the navigator's position and laid out his maps on the small plotting table.

The passengers made themselves as comfortable as possible as the aircraft taxied out on schedule. Armstrong ran up the engines to full power at the end of the runway, pulled back the throttles so that the motors idled for a few moments, then opened up to take-off r.p.m., released the brakes and let the Hudson have her head. After a few seconds the rumble of its undercarriage ceased as Armstrong lifted it from the runway with a steady backward pressure on the control column. He turned on to the heading Kalinski had given him as the Hudson crossed the coast and climbed steadily towards the selected altitude of 15,000 feet, the height from which the bombers would be making their diversionary attack.

They flew on over the Channel, and as the enemy coast drew closer Armstrong was beginning to worry in case the bombers had let them down, even though he reassured himself that there were still five minutes to go before the attack went in as planned. Then, right on cue, searchlights stabbed the sky over Le Havre and Cherbourg, at opposite ends of the Seine Bay.

"Very obliging of them," Kalinski commented. "Now we'll go straight between the goalposts."

Armstrong pointed the Hudson's nose at the darkened coastline midway between the two French ports, above each of which a fierce flak barrage was rending the sky. He could see the twinkling flashes of bomb bursts on the ground. As the coast crawled under the Hudson's wings he called Wilson over the intercom.

"Tell the passengers I'll be starting a rapid descent shortly. Use sign language if you have to. Try to make them understand that if their ears pop, they have to hold their noses and blow."

"Very well, sir," the radio specialist said politely. "But

sign language won't be necessary. I speak quite passable French."

"You might have told us that earlier," Kalinski grunted from the nose. "You could have saved me a trip."

"All right, let's get on with it," Armstrong ordered as the Hudson began to lose height. "You'd better start your running commentary, Stan."

From now on, the success of the mission would depend on Kalinski's map-reading skill as he led the pilot from one landmark to another.

"Okay," the Pole said, "I've got it. Caen is dead ahead. Don't go below three thousand feet, skipper; there's quite a lot of high ground beyond."

Following Kalinski's instructions precisely, Armstrong made a detour around Caen and, picking up the grey, winding ribbon of the river Orne, followed it southwards for twenty miles until Kalinski located a railway line that also ran conveniently southwards through Mayenne to Laval, where he instructed the pilot to turn right on to a new heading of two eight zero degrees.

"Ninety miles to the landing ground," Kalinski announced. "Rennes should be coming up in thirteen minutes."

The Pole was only seconds out in his estimate as the Hudson thundered past Rennes, where the blackout was practically non-existent. In fact, Armstrong had noticed, it had been poor all along the route. The Germans might have succeeded in imposing a strict curfew during the ten months of their occupation, but they had not succeeded in compelling the French citizens to extinguish their lights. It was, he realised, a small gesture of defiance, but a far from insignificant one when it came to RAF aircrews navigating to their targets with the help of these small beacons scattered over France.

The unmasked lights of vehicles, too, helped Kalinski to pick out the road that ran westwards, the road that would lead them to their objective. He was grateful for the unwitting help of these unknown drivers, for the road passed through wooded country and in places it was difficult to detect. He continued to transmit a steady stream of position fixes to the pilot, counting off the miles to the landing zone as he did so.

Suddenly, as the woods slowly petered out, Kalinski made out a confluence of roads, dim in the darkness. Urgently, he told Armstrong, "We're over Loudeac. The small town, right under the nose. The reservoir is dead ahead at six miles. You should see it at any moment."

Armstrong stared into the night, trying to make his eyes relax, searching for the glint of water that would betray the reservoir's position. After a few nervous seconds he saw it, exactly where Kalinski had said it would be. He flew directly over it and then made a right-handed turn to the north, looking down for a sign of the lights that would guide him down to land, but the blackness below remained unbroken.

Damn, thought Armstrong, we could have done with a moon to lighten things up a bit. He prayed that nothing had happened to the 'reception committee'. For the mission to be aborted, especially after Kalinski's magnificent effort in getting to the objective right on schedule, would be a tragedy. But he couldn't go on swanning around the sky for much longer. The Hudson's distinctly non-Germanic engine sound must surely have alerted the enemy, or at least any pro-German French police in the area, by this time.

Kalinski, too, was concentrating on the ground as carefully as he knew how. After a few more tense minutes, his persistence was rewarded by the sight of a red light ahead and off to the left. It flickered on and off in a series of dots and dashes.

Armstrong saw it too, and with relief surging through him he turned the Hudson towards the flickering signal and flashed the aircraft's navigation lights in response. A few moments later, two parallel lines of glowing dots appeared against the dark backdrop of the earth.

The flarepath seemed ridiculously small. This landing, the pilot knew, was going to need every ounce of his accumulated skill. He made a last call over the intercom, telling Wilson to make sure that the passengers were firmly strapped in.

"Right, here we go, then." Gently, Armstrong eased the Hudson round until it was in line with the improvised flarepath, landing into wind. They already knew which direction the wind was coming from at ground level, for Kalinski had been checking it throughout the flight by reference to chimney smoke, but the pilot saw with satisfaction that the reception committee had placed an additional flare at the upwind end of the strip. He suspected, although he could not see, that it also marked the boundary of the landing ground, which was useful to know.

He lowered the undercarriage and flaps and throttled back gradually, allowing the Hudson to sink towards the flarepath, ready to open the throttles again instantly if some unexpected obstacle loomed up out of the darkness. But the reception committee had done its work well and the approach to land was faultless and trouble-free, the flarepath seeming to expand and meet the Hudson as it sank through the last fifty feet. The pilot checked its sink rate with a gentle backward pressure on the stick and, with the flares rushing past the wingtips, allowed it to stall onto the ground.

The undercarriage hit the earth with a thud that rattled the entire aircraft. The Hudson bounced a little way into the air and the pilot fought to keep the wings level as it settled again. This time it stayed down, the pilot ruddering to keep it straight and applying the brakes cautiously. Mud or water, possibly both, splattered against the fuselage. The flares rushed past, then slid by more slowly as the Hudson lost momentum and finally stopped altogether, its engines ticking over. A collective sigh sounded in the cabin as the passengers expelled their pent-up breath.

Kalinski left his position in the nose and hurried back into the cabin, unlatching the main fuselage door. The passengers, with a little help from Wilson, unfastened their seat belts, made for the door and tumbled out into the night. A couple were immediately sick. Kalinski looked on in sympathy; he knew that quite apart from the usual turbulence, sickness in an aircraft could be brought on by the smell of its interior, a mixture of aluminium, cellulose paint, oil and fuel.

The Pole stuck his head outside, inhaling the fresh breeze that held a strong scent of churned-up earth. Wilson joined him.

"I say, would you give me a hand with the passengers' equipment? They seem to have forgotten it in their rush to get out."

Kalinski jumped down from the hatch and helped to unload some suitcases, handing them to the erstwhile passengers. He could see the reception committee, dim shapes in the darkness, standing some distance away. Suddenly, a figure detached itself and approached the aircraft.

"Well done, old chap," it said in extremely cultured English tones. "You'd better be off now. Jolly good effort." The man turned away without another word, leaving Kalinski open-mouthed.

Pulling himself together, he ducked back inside the aircraft and hastened back to the cockpit.

"That's it," he shouted into Armstrong's ear as he went past. "Let's get out of here."

The pilot nodded and opened the throttles, intending to turn the aircraft round and taxi back to the downwind end of the flarepath prior to his take-off run.

The Hudson shuddered, but refused to move. The engines were making enough racket to awaken the dead.

"Bugger it," Armstrong said over the intercom. "We're stuck. She's going to need a shove to free her. Jump out and trap our friends before they disappear, Stan." He throttled back and the roar of the engines died away to a rumble.

Kalinski was out of the aircraft in record time. He ran

to catch up with the Frenchmen, who were making for a copse some distance away. They stopped at his shout and he breathlessly explained the situation to them. Returning to the aircraft, the Frenchmen – there were about a dozen of them, in addition to the mysterious Englishman – clustered around the Hudson and laid willing hands on it at points indicated by the Polish officer, who now jumped back on board. The pilot gunned the engines again, showering his helpers with mud as they pushed with all their strength.

After a couple of minutes, it was apparent that the Hudson was not going to come free. The wheels were sinking deeper into the waterlogged ground. At length, the pilot shut down the engines altogether and climbed down from the aircraft.

"It's no use," he said dejectedly. "She's bogged, and no mistake. Anyone got any bright ideas?"

The cultured Englishman spoke rapidly to the reception committee, some of whom immediately turned and ran off into the night.

"They've gone to get shovels," he explained. "They always bring some with them in case it proves necessary to bury equipment. We'll have a go at digging you out."

"That's fine," Armstrong said with considerable relief, "but I don't think I can risk giving it much more than half an hour. If we haven't got clear of the mud at the end of that time I shall have to set fire to the aircraft and we'll have to take our chances." Uppermost in his mind was the special radio equipment installed in the Hudson; it would be his first duty to ensure that it was destroyed completely.

A few minutes later, the Frenchmen returned with the shovels and a couple of picks, which they immediately applied to the mushy ground in an effort to dig shallow, sloping trenches to front and rear of the Hudson's main undercarriage. It was difficult work in the darkness, especially as the trenches rapidly began to fill up with water. After a while Armstrong, afraid that one of the picks might pierce a tyre, called a halt.

"I'm afraid it's hopeless," he said. "Look – she's sinking even deeper. The bottom of the fuselage is just about resting on the ground. I'm just going to have to burn her," he ended mournfully.

Suddenly, a warning shout came from one of the Frenchmen, who had been acting as lookout and who thought he had seen some movement beyond the flarepath. He was right – in the flickering light of the flares, some figures approached cautiously. The lookout, gun at the ready, ordered them to put up their hands and come closer. Whoever they were, Armstrong thought, it was apparent that they were not Germans.

They turned out to be men from a nearby village. Alerted by the roar of the Hudson's engines, they had defied the local curfew to see what was going on. One of the reception committee spoke to them in low and urgent tones, and after a couple of minutes they hurried off.

"That's a stroke of luck," said Kalinski, who had been listening to the conversation. They've gone to fetch some horses and oxen. They say they'll be back inside an hour."

"All this is making us damnably late," the Englishman

interjected, "but I don't see what else is to be done. We want to get you away from here. The last thing we want is you chaps roaming the countryside; you're bound to be nabbed sooner or later, and I'm afraid we don't have the facilities to hide you or to help you in evading capture. If it hadn't been for a blasted rainstorm earlier on, the ground would have been all right, I'm certain of that."

Armstrong nodded. "Right. But let's get these flares extinguished until the villagers come back. If anything flies overhead, we'll be spotted for sure."

He resigned himself to what seemed an interminable wait, trying vainly to relax, dying for a smoke. Every small night sound made his nerves jump, and his eyes began to ache and smart with the effort of peering into the shadows. The minutes, ticked off by the luminous hands of his wristwatch, crawled around the dial with the speed of a lame snail.

Kalinski, who had exceptionally keen hearing, was the first to detect the jingle of harness, and alerted the others. Suddenly, at the edge of the landing ground, a light flared, followed by another and another.

"Oh, my God," Armstrong groaned, "They've lit torches! What the hell do they think this is – bonfire night?"

"It will be, if we don't get the Hudson out of the shit," remarked Kalinski, whose already excellent command of English had been greatly enhanced by a collection of four-letter words. "Anyway, they must be pretty certain there are no Germans around."

They watched the approaching cavalcade. It seemed almost that the whole village had turned out to help.

The two groups of Frenchmen greeted each other with much handshaking and back-slapping. The throng milled around the stranded Hudson for a while, then sorted itself out into some kind of order; a team of draught horses was harnessed to the undercarriage legs, and the work of freeing the aircraft began once more.

Despite the efforts of men and animals, it was another thirty minutes before the Hudson finally came clear of the mud with a huge sucking sound.

After a brief exchange of farewells the crew lost no time in boarding the aircraft, the Frenchmen scattering to relight the flarepatch as the horses were unharnessed. The Hudson's engines coughed into life and the aircraft began to move, the pilot turning cautiously and starting his taxi run to the downwind end of the flarepath. A group of Frenchmen completed their task of filling in the holes which the Hudson's wheels had dug into the ground, and ran clear as the pilot revved his engines up to full power.

Armstrong released the brakes and the aircraft began to gather speed, its momentum slowed by the weight of the thrown-up mud that caked it. Halfway down the strip, with the tailwheel only just clear of the ground, Armstrong felt with sickening certainty that he was not going to make it. The Hudson's take-off speed was ninety miles per hour, and with the flare that marked the far boundary rushing closer, the airspeed indicator showed only fifty.

Then the miracle happened. The Hudson hit a bump and lurched into the air. Somehow the pilot kept it flying, teetering on the edge of a stall, and flew between two trees at the far end of the field. There was a crunch as its wingtip sliced through some branches, and then it was climbing away into the night.

A plaintive voice sounded over the intercom from the wireless operator's station.

"I say, I felt a little bump. Did we hit something?"

The response that came from the navigator's position was in Kalinski's native Polish, but its tone left Wilson in no doubt that the message was extremely rude.

Chapter Eight

"You gave us a bit of a fright, Ken," Air Commodore Glendenning said. "Thought you weren't going to make it."

"So did we, sir. It was touch and go on take-off. Really close. This close, in fact."

He delved into his tunic pocket and produced a piece of twig, with a leaf still attached to it, and laid it on the air commodore's desk top.

"A piece of the French countryside," he explained. "I knew we'd hit some trees as we took off, but I didn't know we'd brought a branch back with us, embedded in the wingtip." He retrieved the twig and put it back in his pocket: it was going to be his inseparable companion from now on, a reminder of the night when fortune had smiled.

"Well," Glendenning said, "I can tell you that your mission was a complete success. I have Pilot Officer Wilson's report here; it states that he was able to establish clear contact with the French operatives in the course of your return flight."

Armstrong and Kalinski, who was also present, both looked perplexed. The bespectacled radio specialist had said nothing to either of them. Armstrong coughed politely and said, "Are we permitted to know more about all this, sir?"

Glendenning nodded. "Yes, that's why I asked you to come here. I expect you've already guessed that the agents you delivered to France have the priority task of keeping a watch on the German warships in Brest. They also have the secondary task of monitoring other German naval movements in the Biscay area. In order to do this efficiently, we needed to equip them with an effective means of communication with us. Morse transmissions in the high frequency band are slow and too easily detectable, so a very high frequency system has been devised whereby they can communicate directly by voice – in code, of course – with a receiver aircraft flying at altitude over the Channel. Thanks to you, and to Wilson's efforts, this system has now been proved."

The air commodore gave one of his rare smiles. "I expect you were rather puzzled by Wilson. Actually, he invented the system. He's one of the key boffins at the Telecommunications Research Establishment.

"Our eventual aim," the air commodore continued, "is to form a special squadron whose sole task will be to support anti-German resistance movements on the Continent. It will be controlled by an organisation known as the Special Operations Executive, set up on the orders of the Prime Minister. Its function, in Mr Churchill's own words, is 'to set Europe ablaze'. You may yet have a part to play in these operations, Ken."

Glendenning changed the subject abruptly, opening a

folder that lay on the desk in front of him. Armstrong knew that it contained the report he had painstakingly compiled over the previous months, detailing the new techniques and operational procedures developed by his special duties squadron. Some, like the catapult fighter concept, were already in operation, although the 'catafighters', as they were known, had yet to score a success.

Glendenning tapped the folder with his index finger. "It seems to me that two recommendations in your report stand out, Ken, because they can be implemented more or less immediately. The first is the potential use of long-range Beaufighters or Westland Whirlwinds against the Focke-Wulf *Kondor* aircraft that continue to give us a great deal of trouble; the second is the use of very long-range aircraft to patrol the mid-Atlantic gap where our convoys are very much at the mercy of enemy submarines. I see that you recommend the American B-24 Liberator as first choice. Why the Liberator, and not one of our own aircraft – say the Halifax?"

Armstrong smiled wryly. "Can you imagine, sir, the fuss that would be made by Bomber Command if we suggested diverting their newest four-engined bomber to support the Navy? To my mind, the Liberator has all the attributes we need – very long endurance and the ability to carry a substantial weapons load – and we already have half a dozen of them, to my mind completely wasted in ferrying stores over the Atlantic."

Glendenning looked at him in surprise. "I didn't know that. You've obviously done your homework. Tell me more."

"They were originally ordered by the French," Armstrong told him, "and when France surrendered they were taken over by the RAF. As a matter of fact, we've had them since last December, when RAF crews picked them up at Montreal. Bomber Command didn't want to know about them because they did not have self-sealing fuel tanks, so they were turned over to Ferry Command."

Armstrong could not blame Bomber Command for its attitude. In the early weeks of the War, when he had accompanied the then Flight Lieutenant David Pittaway in a daylight attack by Wellington bombers on the German naval base at Wilhelmshaven, he had watched one Wellington after another go down in flames because the bombers did not have self-sealing tanks. It had been a bitter lesson.

"I'll look into that right away," Glendenning said. "I'll also look into the possibility of borrowing a couple of Liberators from Bomber Command, but as you say, it will probably be an uphill struggle. Now, what about this long-range fighter idea?"

Armstrong furrowed his brow. "I've thought a good deal about that," he said, "and on balance I think the Beaufighter will be the better aircraft for the job, even though it will mean taking some off night operations. It was precisely for that reason that I suggested the Whirlwind as an alternative. As you know, only one squadron – No. 263 – is using it at the moment, and they've been leading a pretty nomadic existence hopping between various airfields in the south-west on convoy protection duties. The Whirlwind is a nice aeroplane,

101

with a good armament of twenty-millimetre cannon and a range of about a thousand miles, but its Rolls-Royce Peregrine engines are terrible. The 263 Squadron boys are suffering a grim accident rate, and it's mostly to do with engine failure. Unless the Whirlwind could be fitted with Merlin engines – and I'm told that none are available because they're all going into Spitfires and Hurricanes – I wouldn't risk flying over water in it for any length of time, so that virtually rules it out. It's fast, though, and it would probably make a very good fighter-bomber for anti-shipping operations," he added thoughtfully.

"A point worth considering," Glendenning said, scribbling furiously. "But the Beaufighter it is, then. You still have operational control of a Beaufighter trials flight at West Malling, don't you?"

Armstrong shook his head. "No, sir. It was turned over to Fighter Command at the beginning of the year, but it's still at West Malling."

"Very well. I shall arrange for it to be reassigned. Who will be its commander?"

"Flight Lieutenant Kalinski, sir. He undertook most of the trials last winter, developing interception procedures with the new radar equipment."

"Good." Glendenning looked at the Pole, who had a gleam in his eye at the prospect of getting back into real action at the controls of a fighter. "Where would you prefer the flight to be based?"

"Perranporth in Cornwall, sir," Kalinski answered without hesitation. "It is now ready for operational use and is ideally placed for patrols to the south-west of Ireland, which will cover the route taken by the *Kondors* outbound from their Biscay bases. If the aircraft were made available immediately, patrols could begin within the week."

Glendenning smiled to himself. He suspected that the machinery necessary to begin Beaufighter operations from Perranporth had already been set up behind the scenes by Armstrong, in the anticipation that official approval would be forthcoming. Very well, then, he would make sure that matters moved swiftly.

Armstrong cleared his throat. "There is just one other thing, sir."

The air commodore looked at him enquiringly. "Go on?"

"Well, sir, I think Perranporth would make an ideal location for the whole of the special duties unit, at least while operations against the enemy naval effort remain top priority. It's far too decentralised at the moment, with flights and detachments scattered all over the place. It's very difficult to exercise effective command under these circumstances, especially if something has to be done at short notice, and I'm wasting far too much time flying around the country on the necessary visits."

"Just a moment." Glendenning reached for one of the battery of telephones on his desk, and was soon speaking to a colleague in the Air Staff Directorate of Operations. There followed a wait of a minute or two, then Glendenning thanked whoever was on the other end of the line and replaced the receiver.

"I hope you two can get on with the single-engined fighter boys," he said. "The only unit scheduled for an immediate move to Perranporth is 66 Squadron, whose

Spitfires will be flying in from Exeter in about a week's time. That will leave plenty of room for you, although I should warn you that you might have to operate for at least part of the time from Portreath or Predannack, because Fighter Command's convoy protection operations will take priority and they may have to reinforce Perranporth from time to time. You can get cracking with the move right away, if you like; I'll follow up with the necessary paperwork."

Glendenning provided a staff car to take Armstrong and Kalinski to Croydon, where they had left their Harvard after flying over from Tangmere. They remained at the latter station overnight, collected their kit and, as soon as possible after breakfast, set off for Perranporth.

It was a pleasant flight along the south coast, under a sky dappled with spring clouds that danced along before a westerly breeze, their track taking them over Bournemouth and Lyme Bay before crossing Devon, eventually sighting their destination airfield on the north coast of Cornwall. The newly-built airfield had three good runways joined by a perimeter track; blast pens, each able to shelter two aircraft, led off the latter. Perranporth had originally been opened as a satellite for Portreath, although other uses were now to be found for it. There was one large hangar and several smaller ones, a Watch Office, some flight huts and a Motor Transport Section housed in what had once been an explosives factory that had served the needs of tin mines in the area.

Armstrong landed, checked in at the Watch Office, then he and Kalinski headed straight for one of the flight huts.

Armstrong opened the door and entered a room that smelled of oilcloth and paint.

"Have you got the kettle on, Briggsie?" he shouted.

A door at the end of the room opened and a tall, gangling flying officer entered the room. James MacAlastair Briggs, Armstrong's Adjutant, looked every inch a college lecturer, which is exactly what he had been before the War overtook him. He was an administrator of exceptional efficiency, and Armstrong knew that he was lucky to have him.

"Yes, sir. I saw you coming in." The Adjutant's tone was mournful, in keeping with the expression on his thin features.

"All right, Briggsie, what's up?" Armstrong wanted to know.

"It's this place, sir," Briggs protested. "It's awfully bleak, to say the least. And there are no stoves in the offices or the flight huts. You can't even take a stroll along the clifftop for fear of being blown off your feet, and it's a three hundred foot drop."

"Oh, cheer up," Armstrong said. "There'll be warmer weather along soon. Anyway, you'll soon be too busy to worry about feeling chilly, and I expect the stoves will arrive in due course. Meanwhile, where's that cuppa?"

Briggs told the two pilots that he had managed to fix up accommodation for the squadron's personnel in an hotel in Newquay, some five miles up the road. It was not a particularly satisfactory arrangement, he admitted, and he was trying to organise something nearer the aerodrome, but there were a lot of troops in the area and accommodation was in great demand. It was the best that could be done for the time being.

"Don't worry about it, Briggsie," Armstrong said reassuringly. "I'm sure it will be fine."

In fact, the hotel was more than fine; it was splendid. A large white building with a concave facade, it commanded a fine view over Fistral Bay. Apart from the land mass of Ireland to the north-west, the next land, if one continued due west, was North America.

The hotel, Armstrong learned, was run by identical twin brothers, little tubby bachelors who wore identical black suits, identical bow ties and identical patent leather shoes. Perhaps predictably, they were nicknamed Tweedledum and Tweedledee. They were detested, uniformly and without exception, by every military occupant of the hotel. Only two elderly lady residents, who had refused to leave the place that had become their home under any circumstances, treated them with deference.

Many of the hotel's occupants, Armstrong found to his surprise, were Canadians – officers of the 1st Canadian Division, which had been hurriedly landed in France a couple of weeks before the armistice and just as hurriedly evacuated again. The Canadian Division now formed part of Britain's coastal defences, and from top to bottom it was fed up, as Armstrong and Kalinski discovered when they shared a breakfast table with some of the officers on their first morning in the hotel. One major, whose name of Grant McKenzie clearly betrayed his ethnic origins, expressed the general air of discontent.

"What we want," he said, "is to be part of those British

commando forces. We came over here for action, and we aren't getting any. Nobody is taking any notice of us. It seems we're a kind of embarrassment. Hell's teeth, anything would be better than this. There's no decent food, no decent drink, and the miserable bastards that run this place are straight out of Charles Dickens."

His voice was loud. The two elderly ladies, who had been finishing their breakfast in a corner of the dining room, eager to escape before the influx of what they deemed to be the brutal licentious soldiery, looked scandalised and made their exit. Armstrong felt sorry for them; their world would never be the same again.

Armstrong felt sympathy for the men from across the Atlantic, too, especially since many of their countrymen were already in action in the air; but the threat of invasion, although it appeared to have receded, had not vanished altogether, and even one Canadian division was a valuable asset to Britain's defences. To turn England into an impregnable fortress was the first priority; then, from behind its ramparts, offensive operations could begin.

And Britain could never be an impregnable fortress while mighty German warships and ocean-going submarines roamed the seas, preying on her lifelines.

The Beaufighter flight from West Malling arrived at Perranporth on the twenty-second day of April, a Monday. It comprised four aircraft, still bearing their black night-fighter camouflage, and was commanded by a large, cheerful Irishman called Eamonn O'Day. A flight lieutenant, he was a recent addition to the special duties squadron, selected personally by Armstrong because he was one of the few pilots to have achieved successes against German night bombers while flying Bristol Blenheims. His radar operator was Warrant Officer Phil Kershaw, who had been Armstrong's gunner during the early days of night intruder operations, also on Blenheims, before the Beaufighter had come along.

O'Day and Kershaw, who was probably the RAF's most experienced radar operator, made a formidable team. They had already knocked four German night bombers out of the sky on the approaches to London, and had been fair set to increase their score when the order to move to Perranporth had come through. If they were disappointed, neither of them showed it.

The next day, Flying Officer Piet Van Berg also arrived with his Hurricane flight from Eastchurch, and that afternoon a Handley Page Harrow transport aircraft flew down from Crosby-on-Eden, carrying the squadron's administrative staff and Dickie Baird, who had been tying up the loose ends. Somehow, thanks to Brigg's organisational skills, niches were found for everything – aircraft and personnel alike. That Tuesday night, Armstrong went to bed much contented. The secret squadron was at last beginning to take shape.

Chapter Nine

Bordeaux-Merignac Airfield –
Saturday, 26 April 1941

The early morning throbbed with the sound of engines. In front of the hangars, ground crews busied themselves around four Focke-Wulf *Kondors*, running up their motors, checking equipment, loading bombs and drums of ammunition, making sure that each aircraft's tanks were correctly filled with 2,000 gallons of petrol, the maximum load.

From a safe distance, the aircrews – twenty-four men in all – enjoyed a last smoke before take-off. Two men stood a little apart: they were *Hauptmann* Fritz Meister, officer commanding No. 1 *Gruppe* of *Kampfgeschwader* 40, and his most senior subordinate pilot, *Oberleutnant* Rudolf Riedel, who was also a close friend and his co-pilot.

"What are you thinking, Rudi?" Meister asked suddenly, conscious that his companion was wearing a thoughtful expression. The other started and tossed down his cigar butt, grinding it to extinction with the heel of his flying boot.

"Oh, I was anticipating the future," Riedel answered.

"The *Kondor* has done a fantastic job. After all, it's only a converted airliner. I just wish it had a bigger bomb load. A thousand kilos isn't a lot. I was just imagining how many more ships we'll be able to send to the bottom when its replacement comes along."

Meister gave a grunt. "Anticipation can be a dangerous thing, Rudi," was all he said. He knew something that Riedel did not: the aircraft scheduled to replace the *Kondor*, the Heinkel 177, was still a long way from entering squadron service, even though it had first flown in 1939.

The Heinkel 177 had been plagued with problems from the outset. First of all, it had been subjected to a ridiculous Air Staff requirement that insisted on every new bomber, even one of its size, being stressed for dive-bombing operations, with the result that it was much heavier than originally intended. Then there were the engines. Although the He 177 was a four-engined aircraft, Heinkel, instead of mounting the engines individually on the wing, had taken the radical decision to couple them in pairs, each pair in a single nacelle, driving a single propeller.

There had been a clear indication of the trouble to come when the first flight of the prototype had had to be curtailed when the engines overheated. Although several prototypes were now flying, the engine problems had not yet been overcome and Meister thought that it would be at least another year before the type was fit for operational use.

In the meantime, KG40 – the *Luftwaffe*'s only long-range bomber and maritime patrol unit – would continue to use its handful of *Kondors*, aircraft originally designed as

26-passenger commercial transports for *Lufthansa*, the German airline.

Today's mission was to follow a classic pattern. The five bombers were to attack a small British convoy approaching the west of Ireland, then continue on to Stavanger, in Norway. They would remain there for a day or two, waiting for information on the movements of other British convoys, then return to Bordeaux, making a second attack en route.

Sometimes, KG40's operations took it further south. Only a few days earlier, the *Kondors* had intercepted a convoy between Portugal and the Azores, bound for England from Gibraltar, its presence betrayed by a shadowing U-boat. The *Kondors* had sunk five vessels, the U-boat three more.

The NCO in charge of the ground crews, an *Oberfeldwebel* who had been assigned to KG40 ever since its formation, came up to Meister and saluted.

"*Herr Hauptmann*, I beg to report that everything is ready, and that all the aircraft are fully serviceable."

Meister thanked him in friendly fashion, observing none of the cold aloofness that some officers displayed in their relations with other ranks. His life, and the lives of all his crews, depended on the skill and dedication of such mechanics, who were known affectionately to the flying personnel as *Schwarze* – 'Blackies' – because of the oil that stained their overalls and hands.

The bombers took off at five-minute intervals, heading individually out over the Atlantic. Each aircraft carried a crew of six: two pilots, a navigator, a radio operator, a flight engineer and a rear gunner. Once en route, the radio operators were able to pick up coded signals from a U-boat shadowing the convoy, constantly updating its position.

Skirting the southern tip of neutral Ireland, the Focke-Wulfs altered course to the north, and had already been airborne for several hours when Meister, in the leading aircraft, sighted the convoy in the vicinity of the Rockall Deep. He counted a dozen merchant vessels, escorted by a couple of elderly destroyers – American warships supplied to the Royal Navy, judging by their four funnels – and informed the aircraft that were following.

On Meister's orders, the navigator left his station to man the 20-mm cannon in the nose, while the radio operator took up position behind the MG15 machine-gun in the ventral gondola. Selecting what looked like an oil tanker, the pilot began a rapid descent, levelling out at a very low level over the sea and turning in to make a beam attack on the vessel. He had no other alternative – the *Kondor* was fitted with only a rudimentary bombsight, which ruled out attacks from medium or high level if there was to be any hope of success.

The black bulk of the tanker was silhouetted clearly against the horizon. Meister went for it at full throttle, the airspeed indicator showing over 300 kilometres per hour. He increased height slightly to forty-five metres, the optimum for this kind of attack. Correct altitude was a crucial factor, for in the first three seconds after release the bombs would fall five, fifteen and twenty-five metres – forty-five in total; in that time the bomber would have covered 240 metres, so that was precisely the distance from the target from which the bombs had to be released.

Dropping the bombs was the co-pilot's responsibility. While Meister steered the aircraft directly towards the tanker's superstructure, he remained glued to the bomb-sight, coolly awaiting his moment as the *Kondor* sped over the water at eighty metres per second.

At exactly the right moment he pressed the bomb release and the aircraft's four 250-kilo bombs dropped away in rapid succession, curving down towards the ship in a gentle arc. In the nose, the navigator was blazing away with his cannon, raking the tanker's decks, concentrating on a single gun mounting on the ship's forecastle.

The *Kondor* thundered over the tanker's deck and now the ventral gunner opened up, his bullets sweeping across the ship's superstructure. He saw a splash in the sea that indicated a near miss by one of the bombs, but that was all: the other three were squarely on target. There was no immediate explosion, for the missiles were fused to explode after an eight-second delay to enable the aircraft to get clear.

After leap-frogging the ship, Meister took the *Kondor* down to sea level again and held it there until he was clear of the convoy. The rear gunner reported that the destroyers were putting up flak, but that it was inaccurate. Then, excitedly, he told the crew that the tanker had exploded.

Meister turned the big aircaft, climbing as he did so. The stricken tanker, a vessel of around 8,000 tons, was already surrounded by a sea of blazing fuel oil, from which a mushroom of thick black smoke ascended. As he watched, the ship broke in two. Racked by further explosions, bow and stern slid below the waves with a speed that was terrifying.

Such a sight always sent a chill along Meister's spine, and he forced himself not to think about the luckless men on the doomed tanker.

He went on circling the convoy while the other three aircraft made their attacks, directing them on to the most important targets, and within minutes three more ships were ablaze and sinking. As the bombers droned away into the northern sky, the escorting destroyers set about the task of picking up survivors, their crews only too conscious of how impotent they had been in averting the disaster.

Unknown to the naval gunners, however, they had scored a success. A hundred miles north of the convoy, the crew of the fourth and last *Kondor* to make its attack reported that the aircraft had sustained flak damage and was leaking fuel from the wing tanks. The aircraft was past its point of no return, leaving the crew with no alternative but to fly on in the hope of reaching Stavanger, or to turn back and make an emergency landing in Ireland, where they would be interned for the duration of the War.

Half an hour later, the fuel loss was so bad that the pilot knew that returning to Ireland was his only option; as it was, he would barely make it. Signalling his intention to Meister, he turned the big aircraft round through 180 degrees and headed south-eastward, making for the coast of Donegal.

About the same time that the *Kondor* reversed its course, a twin-engined Armstrong Whitworth Whitley bomber, converted to the maritime patrol role with RAF Coastal Command, was throbbing its way down the main runway of Limavady aerodrome, near Londonderry. The Whitley's young crew were all auxiliaries, for the aircraft belonged to No. 502 Squadron, Ulster's own squadron of the Auxiliary Air Force. The squadron had been carrying out monotonous and unrewarding anti-submarine patrols off the Irish coast since the outbreak of war.

The pilot lifted the Whitley off the runway and climbed past the range of hills that dominated the airfield circuit; the close proximity of the high ground made Limavady a curious choice for an aerodrome. Perhaps it had been envisaged for only daylight fair-weather operations, the pilot thought, but things were different now. Coastal Command flew in all weathers, and it was small wonder that the 1,260-foot peak of Binevanagh, dominating the high ground, was referred to by the aircrews as 'Ben Twitch'.

The pilot climbed to 8,000 feet and his navigator gave him a course to steer for Rockall, the remote outcrop jutting out of the Atlantic 200 miles north-west of Ireland. There, he would turn and fly a series of square search patterns, each one overlapping the other, gradually creeping closer to the Irish coast.

Visibility was good, and for once the pilot was enjoying the flight. All too often, these patrols were flown in rain and cloud, with sudden Atlantic squalls bringing visibility down to zero. But Coastal Command's Whitleys now had the means of penetrating bad weather – the electronic eyes of their air-to-surface radar equipment, known as ASV Mk

II, which could search ten miles ahead and twenty miles on either side. It gave them a fighting chance of getting close enough to a U-boat to make a damaging attack.

The Whitley was about halfway to its first turning point when the rear gunner's voice sounded over the intercom.

"Skipper, there's an aircraft about two miles dead astern, flying north-south, low down. Four engines . . ." His voice rose in excitement. "My stars, I think it's a Focke-Wulf!"

The pilot swore and pulled the Whitley round in a laborious turn, for it was a large aircraft, and far from manoeuvrable. He wondered how he had missed seeing the other aircraft; maybe it had been obscured by the Whitley's starboard wing.

It was a *Kondor* all right – there was no mistaking it. It would have been a sitting target for fighters, as it was well within range of the Irish coast, but the fighter squadrons in Northern Ireland were all in the Belfast area, which was miles away. The pilot made up his mind.

"Let's have a crack at it," he said. "George" – this to the radio operator – "get on the front gun."

The radio operator acknowledged and scrambled into the nose position, settling himself behind the solitary Vickers .303 machine-gun that was the Whitley's nose armament. By way of contrast, the rear gunner had a battery of four similar weapons at his disposal.

The pilot turned in behind the receding Focke-Wulf and put the Whitley into a shallow dive. With a full load of depth charges adding to the aircraft's weight its speed built up rapidly and it quickly overhauled its quarry.

"I'm going to make a run past it," the pilot said, raising his voice to make himself heard over the vibration that was shaking the Whitley, accompanied by a whistle of airflow and some very alarming creakings and groanings. He could now see that the *Kondor* was leaving a thin white trail, which he guessed was fuel. The German aircraft was flying slowly, which seemed to indicate that its pilot was doing his best to conserve whatever fuel remained.

I think he's making for the Free State, the Whitley pilot said to himself. Well, let's see if we can ruin his day for him.

"George, open fire as soon as you're within range," the pilot ordered. "Paddy, as soon as we're abeam I'll drop a wing and give you a clear field of fire. Give the bastard everything you've got."

"It'll be a pleasure, skip," the rear gunner acknowledged, and prepared to do his best.

Almost immediately, the front gun began to chatter and a stream of grey smoke interspersed with glowing tracer rounds reached out towards the Focke-Wulf. The German bomber was flying at a very low altitude and the bullets, falling short at first, carved a white track of foam across the green-grey sea before they disappeared into its starboard wing root. The front gunner kept on firing until the two bombers drew abreast of one another, then was forced to stop because his gun would not traverse any further to the left.

The Whitley pilot turned the control wheel and his left wing dipped towards the sea. At the rear of the aircraft the gunner, his turret turned hard to his right, opened fire in turn, his bullets punching visible holes in the dark green camouflage of the *Kondor*'s upper surfaces. Even as he fired, the gunner wondered why no one on the German aircraft was shooting back; he could not know that all the guns and ammunition on the Focke-Wulf had been jettisoned overboard to lighten it, and that it was utterly defenceless . . .

When the end came, it was surprisingly quick. Without warning, the *Kondor* struck the sea in a splash of foam, bounced several times, and then slewed to a stop, drifting in a nose-down attitude. The Whitley circled the scene, its crew observing that at least some of the Germans had survived the impact; within half a minute a hatch on top of the fuselage was jettisoned and a bundle emerged, followed by three figures. The bundle quickly inflated itself into a rubber life-raft; the three men clung to it but made no attempt to cast it adrift and get into it. They squatted down on top of the fuselage, as though reluctant to leave something that was tangible, and only when the sea was lapping around their feet did they take to the dinghy. As they paddled furiously away, the *Kondor* gradually slipped beneath the waves until only the tail was visible. Then that too was gone, leaving only a tiny orange dot bobbing up and down on the surface of the sea eighty miles from land.

The Whitley pilot told his wireless operator to put out a distress call, together with the position of the dinghy, and toyed with the idea of circling it until rescue arrived; for despite the fact that these were Germans they were fellow airmen, and their enemy now was the sea. Then he told himself that there was a war to be fought, and turned the Whitley back on course for Rockall.

The other three Focke-Wulfs all reached Stavanger safely, but even before they had landed the British 'Y' Service, the organisation responsible for monitoring German low-grade radio transmissions, had been able to formulate a rough idea of KG40's intentions in the immediate future. Their assessment was passed on to the British Admiralty, and Intelligence Officers quickly realised that the bombers' target, on the return flight to Bordeaux, would be Convoy HX121, bound for England from Halifax. On 28 April the convoy, heading for the North Channel that divided western Scotland from Northern Ireland, would be 150 miles out into the Atlantic and passing directly across the track that would be followed by the *Kondors* as they headed for their home base.

There was no time to be lost. By midday on 27 April, Kalinski's Beaufighter flight was on its way from Perranporth to Limavady. From dawn the next day, the crews stood by for action.

Already, at 0200 on the 28th, the 'Y' Service had detected signs that the Germans were preparing for an attack on Convoy HX121. A signal from an enemy submarine, identified as the U-123, had been intercepted during its transmission to German Naval Headquarters; it gave the convoy's current position, and it was intercepted again as it was transmitted from Berlin to KG40's base at Bordeaux. The 'Y' Service operators now monitored the radio frequency used for communications between the Atlantic Air Command in Bordeaux and Stavanger, and at 0400 their vigilance was rewarded. Several bursts of coded letters were detected, logged and deciphered. By 0500, there were clear indications that Convoy HX121 was in imminent danger.

In fact, it was already under attack. Although the U-123, which had been sighted shortly after making its transmission in the early hours of the morning, had been driven off by the convoy escort, contact with HX121 was established some hours later by another submarine, U-96, which closed in and sank two tankers. Two more submarines – the U-65 and U-552 – arrived and attacked in turn, sinking two more ships, but the U-65 was herself sunk by an escorting corvette.

The convoy sailed on, and at Limavady the Beaufighter crews still waited for the call. But as yet – it was now 1400 hours on 28 April – there was no sign of action at Stavanger.

Then, at 1445, a radar outpost on the remote Faeroe Islands detected what appeared to be the movement of two aircraft, possibly more, away to the south-west, towards the Shetlands. The contact was indistinct as the radar was operating at the limit of its range, but a few minutes later a British cruiser, operating between the two groups of islands, confirmed that three *Kondors* had been sighted, heading south-westwards into the Atlantic. Within another thirty minutes, the news had been flashed to Limavady, sending Kalinski and O'Day hurrying to the briefing room, where an Intelligence Officer was waiting for them. Together, they pored over a map of the North Atlantic as he updated them on the convoy's latest position and on the estimated take-off time of the German bombers from Stavanger.

Kalinski made some mental calculations and pointed to a spot on the map. "Assuming the *Kondors* are cruising at about a hundred and seventy miles per hour," he said, "they should intercept the convoy about here. Now, if we can set up a patrol line between St Kilda and Rockall, to the north, we might stand a chance of catching them."

O'Day nodded, making a rough measurement of the distance between the two points with his thumb.

"That's just over two hundred miles," he said. "To be on the safe side, I reckon we should establish the patrol line with three aircraft and set up another one closer to the convoy with the remaining three, which can deal with any of the Huns that manage to break through."

They settled the question of who was going to lead which flight by the simple expedient of tossing a coin, which determined that Kalinski would take care of the outermost patrol line, then settled down to make some finer calculations. Their hopes of intercepting the *Kondors* would depend on a good deal of luck, Kalinski knew, for although the Beaufighter had a respectable combat radius his flight would have enough fuel for only ten or fifteen minutes' patrol time at the outside. O'Day's flight, which would be taking off a few minutes later and which would have less distance to fly, would have a greater fuel margin.

It was now 1615, and time was becoming critical. Kalinski and O'Day hurried back to their dispersal and quickly briefed the other crews, who had been standing by their aircraft, and within minutes Kalinski's flight of three Beaufighters was airborne and climbing into the northern sky.

At that moment, *Hauptmann* Meister's flight of three *Kondors* was exactly over a point in the ocean known as the Rosemary Bank, just over a hundred miles north-west of the Island of Lewis, in the outer Hebrides. From Stavanger, the aircraft had made a lengthy detour around northern Scotland, flying west-north-west for 300 miles before altering course south-west as they passed between the Faeroes and the Shetlands. Now, another 280 miles further on, they altered course again, turning due south. They had already been airborne for close on four hours.

Kalinski's flight reached its patrol line after some forty minutes' flying time and the Beaufighters spread out, each taking a sixty-mile sector. The pilots constantly monitored their fuel gauges, and adding to their concern was the fact that the weather was deteriorating, with cloud spreading from the north-west. Ice was beginning to form on the wings and cockpit canopies of their aircraft. The radar operator in each aircraft was currently acting as an extra pair of eyes, keeping a lookout through the perspex blister on top of the fuselage, behind the pilot's position; if the weather got any worse, they would revert to their radar sets in the hope of picking up a contact.

The minutes ticked by, and Kalinski felt growing despair. The weather continued to worsen, and the fuel state was worrying. At length, he made up his mind and called up the other two pilots, ordering them to return to base. He was not prepared to risk the lives of his crews on what was fast becoming a wild-goose chase.

He turned south and climbed, intent on calling Limavady for a bearing. Suddenly, at 6,000 feet, the Beaufighter popped out of the cloud into red, frosty sunlight.

A huge aircraft hung silhouetted against the sky, a mere 200 yards ahead and a few hundred feet higher up. Kalinski made a note of his heading and dropped back into the cloud again. Quietly, over the intercom, as though afraid of being overheard by the crew of the other aircraft, he said to his radar operator, Sergeant Thomas, "I'm taking her up a bit. Look ahead, and tell me what you see."

Thomas, who had abandoned his visual lookout and who had just seated himself in front of his AI radar set, returned to his perspex blister and peered out as Kalinski cautiously emerged from the cloud again. He could plainly see the white-edged black cross on the other aircraft's fuselage.

"It's a *Kondor* all right," Thomas said.

"Okay. Start tracking him on the AI in case he dives into the cloud."

Kalinski held his position below and behind the German bomber, turned the safety catch of his guns to 'fire' and pressed the button. The Beaufighter shuddered with the recoil as its four cannon and six machine-guns opened up. The vibration caused the silhouette of the aircraft in front to dance and shake. Brilliant flashes flickered over its outline, accompanied by puffs of smoke.

Kalinski went on firing. Pieces from the *Kondor* hurtled back past the Beaufighter, narrowly missing the cockpit, causing the pilot to duck instinctively.

The *Kondor* went into a steep left-handed descending turn and plunged into the cloud. Kalinski fired another burst at it, and an instant later the Beaufighter was rocketing skywards on the shock wave of a terrific explosion. Kalinski temporarily lost control and the fighter stalled. He corrected quickly, bringing the aircraft back to level flight just over the cloud tops. Below, a bright glow faded gradually as the disintegrating wreckage plummeted towards the sea.

"What happened, skipper?" Thomas said breathlessly.

"Must have cooked off his bomb load," the pilot told him. "Anyway, not much doubt about that one." He looked at his fuel state, which was now dangerously low, and throttled back, reducing the setting to economical cruising speed. With luck, they'd just about make it back.

The two remaining Focke-Wulfs, meanwhile – which had become separated from Kalinski's victim and were some minutes ahead of it – flew on towards convoy HX121's last reported position, their crews unaware of the fate of their colleague, or of the fact that they were flying into a trap. In the leading aircraft, Meister felt confident, despite the much-reduced visibility. He was still receiving a steady flow of position reports via Bordeaux, and after the attack the gathering low cloud would provide an excellent refuge for the aircraft.

Meanwhile, O'Day's three Beaufighters had arrived in the vicinity of the convoy to be greeted by a storm of anti-aircraft fire which ceased abruptly as the naval gunnery directors recognised the incoming aircraft as friendly. As planned, the three fighters set up a combat air patrol line some distance to the north of the convoy, O'Day quietly fuming with the realisation that they had narrowly missed being shot out of the sky by their own side.

He would have been even more furious had he realised that for the past ten minutes, the incoming *Kondors* had been tracked by a Type 284 radar installed in one of the convoy's escorting cruisers, but that no means existed for direct communication by radio between the warship and the aircraft.

O'Day had been patrolling for exactly eight minutes when the quiet and confident voice of his radar operator, Kershaw, alerted him to the approach of the enemy aircraft.

"Contact bearing zero-one-zero, three miles, fifteen hundred feet."

"Only one?" the pilot questioned. Kershaw answered in the affirmative. The crews of the two *Kondors*, in fact, had already sighted the convoy's smoke, just visible against the murky horizon, and on Meister's orders had split up to make their attacks from different directions. It was the second aircraft that now showed as a blip on Kershaw's cathode ray tube; an operator of lesser skill might have failed to pick it out at all against the background 'clutter', the reflection from the sea.

A few moments later, O'Day sighted the enemy aircraft and informed Kershaw that he was going to make a head-on attack. Otherwise, by the time he got astern of it, it would be in a position to strike at the convoy. He opened the throttles and raced towards it, thumb poised over the gun button as the *Kondor*'s silhouette grew larger in his sight.

At the last moment, the enemy pilot sighted the peril that was racing headlong towards him and pulled back on the control column, pointing the bomber's nose towards the sheltering clouds. He was too late, and his manoeuvre exposed the bomber's underside to the storm of gunfire that erupted from the Beaufighter. O'Day passed under the stricken Focke-Wulf with feet to spare, smelling its reek of hot oil, then turned hard, intent on making a second attack.

He was in time to see the *Kondor* weaving down towards the sea, trailing a snake of dense black smoke, flames streaming back from ruptured fuel tanks. It turned on its side, one wingtip slicing into the water, and cartwheeled in a cloud of wreckage. All that was left was a circle of burning fuel, surrounded by a few islands of debris. There could have been no survivors.

A couple of miles away, the rear gunner in Meister's aircraft, his voice shaking, reported having seen the destruction of the other *Kondor*. Meister, intent on setting up his attack, selected a large freighter and went down to wave-top level, keeping under the barrage of flak that now filled the sky between the sea and the clouds.

Suddenly, he realised that his rear gunner was firing – at what, he had no idea. Then the sea around the Focke-Wulf exploded in a welter of foam and gaping holes appeared in the bomber's left wing.

"Two fighters behind us!" the rear gunner screamed. His cry was abruptly cut off as cannon shells ripped into his cupola, silencing him for ever. The nose of the bomber began to snake from side to side and the rudder pedals failed to respond to the pressure of Meister's feet, telling him that the tail had sustained damage.

"It's no use, Rudi, I can't hold her straight!" he yelled. *"Bomben los!"*

The co-pilot pulled the bomb release and the missiles fell away to explode harmlessly in the sea. At the same moment, Meister pulled the bomber up into the cloud layer where he levelled out, testing the controls cautiously. The Focke-Wulf was still flying, but only just. He didn't give much for their chances of reaching Bordeaux.

Behind him, O'Day's Beaufighter flight headed for home, low on fuel. On the bridge of the cruiser, a signal lamp winked at them as they departed, flashing 'well done' in Morse.

A few hours later, the surviving ships of Convoy HX121 rounded the northern tip of Ireland and entered the North Channel, sailing on through the Irish Sea and into Liverpool Bay.

Shortly after dropping anchor, one of the escorting corvettes offloaded a pitiful cargo: three German airmen, picked up some time earlier off the north coast of Ireland, where the tides and currents had carried their life-raft. They had been drifting for two days and nights and were in a dreadful condition, more dead than alive. But it would be a long time before they knew just how lucky they really were.

Chapter Ten

*German Naval Staff Headquarters, Berlin –
1 May 1941*

The view from the broad, high windows of the building in the Wilhelmstrasse hardly portrayed a capital city at war. In fact, had it not been for the uniforms in the streets, there was nothing to indicate that Germany was in a state of conflict. Nothing, that was, except for a little bomb damage here and there, caused by those infernal British bombers.

The first British air raid on Berlin, in retaliation for an attack on London in August 1940, had come as a shock to the citizens, especially since the *Luftwaffe* Commander-in-Chief, Hermann Goering, had assured them that no enemy aircraft would ever fly over the territory of the Reich. The raid itself had been laughably ineffective, destroying nothing more than a wooden summerhouse and slightly injuring two people. Most of the bombs had fallen well clear of the city into the agricultural land that supplied most of Berlin's fruit and vegetables. "Now the Tommies are trying to starve us out," the Berliners had jested.

There had been little to joke about on the night of

Fortress England

23 September 1940, however, when over 120 British bombers attacked railway yards, power stations, gasworks and factories in the city. The Moabit district of Berlin, the working-class area that was the equivalent of London's East End, was badly hit, with many people killed and injured. News of the raid was subjected to heavy censorship, and consequently very few people living outside Berlin knew about it. The Berliners themselves, for the first time, began to feel some apprehension, wondering if this was only a foretaste of things to come. But as the months passed, and Berlin was attacked very infrequently by only small numbers of bombers, the apprehension turned to relief, and Berlin went about its normal routine business without interruption.

In any case, Berliners reasoned, the War would soon be over. Britain was isolated, and would soon be starved into submission by the German Navy. In North Africa, the British were reeling under the onslaught of General Rommel's *Afrika Korps*; and in Europe, the swastika flag flew over conquered territories from Norway to the Balkans. All that remained unvanquished was that damned, stubborn little offshore island . . .

A dozen men sat around the polished oak table in the Naval Staff HQ. Presiding over them was *Grossadmiral* Erich Raeder, Commander-in-Chief of the German Navy. Not all were naval officers; among them was *Oberstleutnant* Martin Harlinghausen, the recently appointed *Fliegerfuhrer Atlantik* – Air Commander Atlantic – at Lorient.

The officers, all of senior rank, listened intently as an

Intelligence Officer briefed them on the current naval situation. Raeder knew it already, of course, but it was important to bring the others completely up to date. A slide projector, operated by a senior naval rating, threw an image of the Atlantic Ocean onto a large screen.

The Intelligence Officer began with a summary of U-boat operations in the Atlantic during April, using a long pointer to indicate various areas of ocean.

"At the beginning of the month," he stated, "a patrol line consisting of eight U-boats was formed here, south of Iceland, to intercept a convoy bound for Britain. The engagement began on the second of April, and in the next two days they succeeded in sinking eleven merchant ships. Unfortunately, one of our submarines, *Leutnant* von Hippel's U-76, was also lost, believed sunk by a destroyer. On the thirteenth, *Kapitanleutnant* Scholtz in U-108 sank the British auxiliary cruiser *Rajputana*, a vessel of over sixteen thousand tons, in the Denmark Strait."

There were murmurs of approval. Since the beginning of the War the British had lost thirteen of these vessels, which were fast merchant ships converted for war duty as an answer to Germany's commerce raiders. Without armour protection and under-armed, they were no match for the vessels they were supposed to catch and destroy. In fact, the *Rajputana* was the second auxiliary cruiser to be sunk in April; a few days earlier, the *Voltaire* had been destroyed in the central Atlantic by the raider *Thor*.

"A further patrol line," the Intelligence Officer continued, "was established south of Iceland on the eighteenth, comprising four U-boats and four Italian submarines. A convoy was twice sighted by the Italians, but they failed to direct our U-boats onto it, or to attack it themselves."

There was a snort of derision from one of the naval officers at the table. The Italian boats had been transferred to the French Atlantic ports some months earlier, at a time when the German Navy did not have sufficient U-boats to operate effectively in the Atlantic, and at first they had scored a number of successes; now they were more of a hinderance than a help.

"Finally, towards the end of the month, our submarines and aircraft operated against a convoy bound for England from Nova Scotia and succeeded in sinking a number of vessels, although the air attacks did not go as planned."

"Explain, please," Raeder interrupted sharply.

"If I may be permitted, sir?"

Raeder looked at Harlinghausen, who had just spoken, and nodded. The *Luftwaffe* commander rose and addressed the assembly.

"The plan," he said, "was for the convoy to be attacked by four *Kondors* from Bordeaux. They were to fly to Stavanger, having attacked another, smaller convoy en route, and then strike at the main convoy on their return flight. Unfortunately, something went wrong and one of the aircraft was lost in unknown circumstances on the outward journey. The other three remained at Stavanger for two days, then set out to attack the main convoy as it approached Ireland. It appears that they were intercepted by British fighters: two were shot down and the third – the group commander's aircraft – barely succeeded in reaching

Bordeaux with severe damage to its tail unit and a dead gunner."

"Where exactly were our aircraft when they were intercepted?" Raeder wanted to know. Harlinghausen went over to the screen and pointed to a spot roughly 200 miles north-west of Ireland.

"So," Raeder said thoughtfully, "for reasons of range, that would seem to rule out the possibility that the British fighters were Spitfires or Hurricanes."

"Yes, sir. The crew of the *Kondor* that got away identified them as twin-engined, and said that they were heavily armed. They can only have been Bristol Beaufighters. This is the type which is replacing the Blenheim in the RAF's night-fighter force," Harlinghausen explained.

"Could this have been an accidental interception?" Raeder asked. The *Luftwaffe* officer shook his head.

"We don't think so, sir. We think that the British somehow learned of the *Kondors*' mission, and laid a trap for them."

"Very well," Raeder said, "we shall return to this matter later. Thank you, Harlinghausen." He ordered the Intelligence Officer to continue with his briefing.

"Here are the dispositions of our major warships," the Intelligence Officer went on. "The *Scharnhorst* and *Gneisenau* are still in Brest, where the latter is undergoing repair; the approaches to the harbour have been heavily mined by the enemy, which is causing us some concern. Of the others, the battleships *Admiral Scheer* and *Lutzow* are in Kiel, together with the heavy cruiser *Admiral Hipper*. The other heavy cruiser, the *Prinz Eugen*, is in the Baltic, conducting exercises with the battleship *Bismarck.*"

The Intelligence Officer spent several more minutes talking about the current state of the German Navy, giving details of the estimated tonnages of Allied shipping sunk in April 1941 by submarines, warships and aircraft and concluding with some information which, to at least some of the assembled officers, had alarming indications for the future.

"Some time ago," the Intelligence Officer said, "our embassy in Washington informed us that the United States Government was about to implement a neutrality patrol in the Central Atlantic, operating from Bermuda. This has now been established, gentlemen, and the force deployed consists of an aircraft carrier, two cruisers and two destroyers."

He turned to the projected image of the Atlantic and traced a line down it with his pointer.

"What this means, quite simply, is that any U-boat which attacks the shipping of any neutral country, including the United States, anywhere in the Western Hemisphere beyond this line – Longitude thirty degrees west – is itself liable to be attacked by the United States Navy."

He paused and turned to face his audience again. "And there is more. It appears that during the second week in April, a directive was issued to Headquarters, United States Pacific Fleet, for the transfer to the Atlantic of a further aircraft carrier, three battleships, four cruisers and a number of destroyers. When this transfer will take place we do not yet know, but I am sure you will agree that it is an ominous development. We obviously do not want an armed confrontation on the high seas with the United States of America."

"I agree with you, Riecken." Admiral Raeder rose suddenly, flexing his shoulders to ease a twinge of rheumatism, and moved across to each window in turn, pulling the cords that opened the venetian blinds, which had been closed to dim the room. He opened a window, letting in the warm afternoon air, sniffing the scent of the blossom that rose from the trees in the broad street below him.

Abruptly, he strode back to his place at the head of the table, but remained standing, his hands clasped behind his back. The 65-year-old Grand Admiral bore himself proudly, and there was justification in his pride, for he was the architect of the Third Reich's mighty navy. He believed that powerful surface ships, including aircraft carriers, were the key to victory on the high seas, and in this he was at odds with his subordinate, Admiral Karl Doenitz, who favoured ocean-going submarines as the primary means of attack. Well, Raeder thought as he surveyed the officers at the table, his own ideas were about to be vindicated.

"Gentlemen," he said in a high, clear voice, "I have excellent news. In exactly three weeks' time the most powerful warship afloat, the *Bismarck*, will leave the Baltic and enter the Atlantic Ocean, accompanied by her consort, the *Prinz Eugen*. In due course they will be joined by the *Scharnhorst* and, once the repairs to her are completed, the *Gneisenau*. Never before, in the history of naval warfare, will the world have seen such a mighty concentration of firepower. Supported by our U-boats, these ships will tear

Britain's convoys to shreds. They will sink her best and most modern warships. In short, they will bring Britain to her knees. Within a few months at the outside, the stubborn British will be begging for peace."

If anyone at the table wore a doubtful expression, the enthusiastic *Grossadmiral* never noticed it. And it was perhaps as well that he was not clairvoyant, for had he been able to peer only a week ahead into the future, he might have seen the gigantic spanner that was about to be thrown into the workings of his operational plans.

South of Iceland – Friday, 9 May 1941

It was the second seriously unhappy moment in *Kapitanleutnant* Julius Lemp's career as a naval officer. The first had been on 27 September 1939, only three weeks after the outbreak of war, when he had sailed home to Wilhelmshaven in submarine U-30 to find that, instead of sinking an armed merchant cruiser some 200 miles west of the Hebrides, his victim had been the liner *Athenia*, which had gone down with the loss of 112 passengers and crew out of 1,400. To make matters worse, twenty-eight of the dead were Americans, and it had taken an intense flurry of diplomatic activity between Berlin and Washington to prevent the United States from plunging headlong into the War on Britain's side.

Now, in the third year of the War, Julius Lemp was a leading U-boat 'ace', in command of U-110. For two days he had been closing on a British convoy and at length had successfully engaged it, sinking two ships, but had immediately been forced to the surface following a damaging depth-charge attack. Lemp and his crew were picked up unharmed after a few frightening moments when a British destroyer came charging down on the U-boat, apparently intent on ramming it; the destroyer had sheered off at the last moment, her captain having decided to attempt taking the crippled submarine in tow.

What was troubling Lemp was one simple fact: in the rush to abandon the U-110 the procedure for scuttling the boat, and for destroying the secret equipment on board, had not been carried out. And now, as Lemp and his crew huddled miserably below decks on the destroyer, HMS *Bulldog*, a British boarding party was at work deep in the bowels of the submarine, seeing what they might salvage, painfully conscious that hidden explosive charges might send them to oblivion at any moment.

What they found was to alter the course of the bitter conflict that was fast becoming known as the Battle of the Atlantic. Inside the submarine, with its associated code books, was an Enigma encryption machine. Discovering the code machine was not in itself significant, because the British already possessed a couple, passed on in 1939 by a Polish crypto-analyst. What was significant was that on the machine there was a signal, already set up for transmission. This, together with the code books they also found in the little radio operator's office opposite the captain's quarters, would – for the first time – enable British experts to read at least part of the German Naval Enigma code, which was called the Home Waters setting.

Fortress England

Britain's Government Code and Cypher School now had access to the secrets of the *Kurzsignale*, the short signals in which the U-boats transmitted their sighting reports and weather information. In the weeks to come, the specialists would be able to read all the German U-boat signals traffic, which could be deciphered with only a few hours' delay.

The Home Waters setting of the Enigma cypher, which was changed daily, carried 95 per cent of the German Navy's radio message traffic. The information it yielded, together with that of other enemy high-grade cyphers, became known as Ultra. The whole operation was so vital to Britain's survival that even the name Ultra was classified top secret.

The breakthrough of May 1941 was to move the whole war against the U-boats into a new dimension. The code-breakers and the Admiralty Submarine Tracking Room now had an insight into the whole operational cycle of a U-boat, and although many months were to pass before the Tracking Room could claim to know more about the U-boats' deployment than Admiral Doenitz's own staff, the summer of 1941 was the point at which the Government Code and Cypher School moved the process out of the realms of guesswork. From now on, this knowledge of U-boat movements and positions, derived from Ultra, would enable the Admiralty to reroute convoys to avoid the U-boat packs.

The wolf-pack tactics employed by the U-boats called for the transmission of sighting reports and homing signals between boats so that they could concentrate and attack

137

on the surface at night in areas beyond the range of shore-based aircraft. Convoys were virtually defenceless against these tactics, but their success depended on tightly centralised control by U-boat Command and the transmission of a stream of tactical orders, patrol instructions, situation reports and so on. This made them vulnerable to Ultra and to high-frequency direction finding. Also, Ultra provided huge quantities of valuable background information that included such details as the exit and approach routes from and to the U-boat bases, frequency of patrols and the rate at which new boats were being commissioned. It also revealed operational characteristics such as the speed, diving depths, endurance, armament, signals and radar equipment of the various types of U-boat, and the current operational state of boats at sea.

Admiral Doenitz's U-boat offensive in the spring of 1941 had been launched in the expectation that the previously high rate of merchant ship sinkings could not only be maintained but decisively increased as more submarines were deployed. In this way the German Naval Command hoped to neutralise Britain before help arrived from the United States in significant proportions.

In Whitehall, as the offensive got under way, the outlook was bleak. At the beginning of 1941 food stocks in Britain were dangerously low, and they were severely rationed. There was enough wheat for fifteen weeks; meat for only two weeks; butter for eight weeks; margarine for three weeks; and bacon for twenty-seven weeks. There were no longer any stocks of imported fruit. All this added up to the grim fact that, unless merchant ship sinkings could be reduced, Britain would starve before new merchant vessels could be built fast enough to maintain imports at the level needed for her survival.

The Ultra breakthrough had come only just in time.

Chapter Eleven

Sunday, 4 May 1941: Dawn

It had been a weekend of terror for the city of Liverpool. The attacks of the two previous nights had been bad enough – 48 tons of bombs and 112 canisters of incendiaries had fallen on the city in the first night of May, dropped by 43 German bombers, and on the following night 65 more bombers had caused massive destruction in the city centre.

If the people of Liverpool thought this was bad enough, there was far worse to come. On Saturday night, nine Heinkel 111s of III/KG26 under the command of Major Viktor von Lossberg took off from Poix near Amiens and set course for the city. Each aircraft was equipped with a radio navigation aid called Y-Apparatus; a ground station at Cherbourg transmitted a high-frequency radio beam which the bombers followed. Normally, the 'pathfinder' Heinkels operated at between 9,000 and 12,000 feet, but on this occasion, in order to receive the signals for as long as possible, they went up to 22,000.

Radar tracked them as they crossed the Channel, and as they came in over the south coast the Beaufighters pounced.

One Heinkel fell in flames over Somerset, another broke up in mid-air near Chichester and a third, appropriately, crashed in the Corporation scrapyard at Arundel.

The others flew on, and although the radio signals petered out as the bombers passed over Wrexham, thirty miles south-east of Liverpool, the city was now only seven minutes' flying time away and the crews had no difficulty in locating their objective. Ignoring decoy fires that had been lit on the Dee Estuary, they dropped their loads of incendiaries and then turned away, speeding for the Channel and safety.

Behind them came the main bomber stream: 293 He 111s and Ju 88s of *Luftflotte* 3. Of these, 218 attacked Liverpool, causing huge fires in the docks and sinking several ships.

One ship under attack gave cause for particular concern. She was the SS *Malakand*, and she was laden with 1,000 tons of high-explosive bombs. Soon after the attack started, a partly inflated barrage balloon fell over her deck and started to blaze fiercely. Under the direction of the ship's master, Captain Howard Kinley, the crew managed to bring the fire under control after fifteen minutes, and also dealt with some incendiaries which fell on the vessel. All the while, HE bombs and incendiaries were exploding on the dock sheds nearby.

By midnight, the *Malakand* was surrounded by a sea of flame from burning dockyard buildings on both sides. One huge fire spread to the ship itself and soon enveloped her from stem to stern, forcing the crew to abandon her. They and members of the Auxiliary Fire Service continued to fight the flames all night, but after nine hours there was a massive explosion as part of the vessel's deadly cargo blew up, wrecking the dock and completing the destruction, already begun by the *Luftwaffe*, of acres of surrounding sheds and warehouses. Steel plates from the stricken ship were later found two and a half miles away. Captain Kinley and several of his crew were injured, but it was a miracle that only four people were killed.

More of the bombs stacked inside the ship's white-hot hulk detonated at intervals over the next three days. Had the whole cargo gone up at once, the devastation and loss of life would have been indescribable.

As it was, 479 people were killed that night in Liverpool and the surrounding area. One large HE bomb fell in the back courtyard of Mill Road Infirmary, completely demolishing three large hospital buildings and damaging the rest; 62 people were killed, half of them patients, and 70 more seriously injured.

The Mersey anti-aircraft barrage hurled 6,000 rounds of heavy shells at the attackers during the night and shot nothing down, although one Heinkel fell victim to a barrage balloon cable. One Junkers 88 had to make a forced landing in Norfolk as a result of engine failure, but of the nine German aircraft that failed to return, seven were brought down by night-fighters, five by Beaufighters and two by Boulton Paul Defiants.

Others had narrow escapes, as one German crew member later described:

'We were over the North Sea when suddenly our

radio operator shouted 'Night fighter!' It was one of their new, very fast fighters. We had hardly grasped the meaning of his words when a hail of bullets was pumped into our aircraft. Indescribable chaos surrounded us immediately. We were blinded by tracer bullets and deafened by the whistle of projectiles.

Our pilot tried an evasive manoeuvre but time and again, with astounding courage and insistence, the excellent enemy pilot pumped more and more lead into us. Six times he attacked us from below, but never allowed his machine to come within the range of our guns.

The bomb-aimer was wounded and lay motionless near his sight. Our pilot attempted once more to shake off the British attacker, diving almost to sea level, and at last succeeded. But one of our motors was out of action. Still, we were now left undisturbed. We jettisoned our bombs, and flew home.

We had great difficulty in dressing the wounds of our comrade in the darkness, but we managed to make a successful landing, and soon our comrade was transferred to hospital. Later, we counted the hits which our machine had sustained. We found no fewer than one hundred and seven holes.'

Other British ports were hit that night. Ten people were killed and 2,000 made homeless in Barrow-in-Furness; casualties were heavy on Tyneside, where a bomb scored a direct hit on an air-raid shelter and killed 76; 20

people lost their lives in attacks on Sunderland and West Hartlepool; and a similar number were killed in raids on Portsmouth and Gosport. But it was Liverpool that suffered the most.

Dawn rose on a devastated city. Its streets were blocked with fallen masonry, carpeted with millions of shards of broken glass and festooned with miles of snaking rubber fire hoses. The air itself seemed somehow altered: sharp and acrid, it stung the eyes and pinched the nostrils. A great pall of smoke and dust hung over everything, and a black blizzard of burnt paper from stricken shops and offices blew across the city to settle in suburban gardens. One eyewitness told how he:

'. . . walked along some of the scores of fissured streets where gas and water mains were ruptured, where sleep-starved rescue teams toiled and scrabbled among rubble that had been homes – streets where people, some very young, some very old, drifted in trauma through a haze of smoke and dust and stench from burst sewers. I saw tortured bodies of carthorses that had been dragged from blazing stables, then abandoned in heaps because there were humans to extricate. I saw shambling cows released by bombs from back-street byres, bellowing to be milked. I saw a baby's body in the splintered debris of its cradle.

I saw some of the many hundreds in Liverpool and in adjoining Bootle who had lost a home and everything in it, those frantic for news of a loved one, those in anguish because they had received it.'

Fortress England

This was Liverpool at daybreak, on Sunday, 4 May 1941.

In contrast to the blood-red sun that glared evilly through the smoke of Liverpool's fires, the morning sun that rose over Bordeaux shone through an atmosphere that was fresh and clean, filled with the song of birds. It was an atmosphere of rural tranquillity that was soon to be abruptly shattered.

Eight aircraft came roaring out of the north-eastern sky, flying in two waves of four. They thundered at low level over Bordeaux-Merignac airfield, then peeled off smartly into the circuit, coming in to land one by one with a precise interval between each. *Oberstleutnant* Martin Harlinghausen, who had travelled down from Lorient to greet the newcomers, smiled his approval.

"Excellent airmanship," he commented. "That is good. A *Staffel* whose discipline is good will fight well. Do you not agree, Fritz?"

Fritz Meister nodded. He was still recovering from the nervous exhaustion caused by the nightmare flight back to Bordeaux a few days earlier, and haunted by the loss of all his aircraft but one.

"They will be a valuable addition to our firepower, *Herr Oberstleutnant*," he said, looking appreciatively at the aircraft as they taxied in. They were Junkers 88s, but there was something different about them. Instead of the transparent noses of the bomber version, these aircraft had 'solid' noses, and the muzzles of cannon and machine-guns protruded from them.

145

They were Ju 88C-2s, originally converted to a fighter configuration for intruder operations over England. Operating from Bordeaux, they would provide an antidote for the RAF's Bristol Beaufighters, which had suddenly begun to appear on patrol off the French coast, ranging as far south as the Bay of Biscay. Nothing else had the necessary combination of range, speed and manoeuvrability to cope with the twin-engined British fighter.

Admiral Raeder, Meister thought, must have pulled numerous strings with his *Luftwaffe* counterparts to have these valuable aircraft assigned to the Atlantic Air Command. But there was more to come.

Even before the crews of the newly-arrived aircraft had shut down their engines at their dispersal points, more aircraft came thundering in from the north. These, too, were Ju 88s, but the standard dive-bomber version. Meister counted eighteen of them as they came in to land, their BMW radial engines making a fearsome racket.

"There you are, Fritz," said Harlinghausen, grinning. "That came as a surprise, didn't it? Now we have real striking power."

Meister glanced sideways at his superior officer. Something was obviously going on that he knew nothing about. All this activity pointed to a massive strengthening of both offensive and defensive capability on the Biscay coast. He wondered if the battlecruisers at Brest were going to break out into the Atlantic under cover of a big air umbrella.

He wished that he could have the opportunity to fly one of the Ju 88 fighters, and take a crack at the Beaufighters which he knew had been responsible for the death of his squadron. The previous evening he had seen photographs, brought back by a reconnaissance aircraft, which had revealed the presence of the British fighters on an airfield in Cornwall, and a German agent in Ireland had signalled their brief visit to an airfield in the north. Now they were back in Cornwall and flying patrols as far out as Biscay. So far, no German aircraft had been lost in this area, but Meister knew with a feeling of unease that if the patrols were allowed to continue unmolested, the anti-shipping Heinkels that formed part of KG40's bomber force at Bordeaux would be in for a hard time. The reinforcement had come not a moment too soon.

Other eyes, too, had witnessed the arrival of the two formations of Ju 88s. That night, from the comparative security of a tiny room hidden in a church steeple in Bordeaux, radio contact would be made with a specially-equipped Hudson which, every night, cruised high over the Channel between certain hours. It formed a vital link in the Intelligence chain which, when forged completely, would give the Allies ascendency in the Atlantic war. Only a handful of people would ever know how vital that link would be.

Chapter Twelve

The Air Ministry, London – Friday, 9 May 1941

"The Prime Minister is very concerned," Air Commodore Glendenning said quietly. "He has an excellent grasp of naval affairs, and he believes this maximum-effort offensive by the Germans is definitely linked to forthcoming operations by their fleet. Almost without exception, their heaviest attacks have been directed against our ports, and they have been in progress all week. Look at the map."

Armstrong did so, noting that a number of points around the coasts of Britain were heavily circled in red. Glendenning pointed to each of them in turn.

"First of all, Liverpool, last Saturday. Then, on Sunday night, Belfast, with secondary attacks on Liverpool and Barrow, not to mention smaller raids around the coast. As far as we can tell, about four hundred and fifty aircraft were involved. The shipyards at Belfast took a real pasting, and we managed to shoot down five aircraft. Five! That's hardly likely to deter them, is it?"

The air commodore's index finger moved eastwards across the Irish Sea.

"On Monday and Tuesday it was Glasgow, with the

Greenock shipyards as the main target area. They were hard hit. Again, there were smaller secondary raids. Anti-Aircraft Command blasted off thousands of rounds, Fighter Command put up three hundred sorties, and we shot down three aircraft. To make the figures even worse, a German intruder shot down one of our Defiants. Luckily, the crew baled out.

"On Wednesday Liverpool and Hull got clobbered – especially Hull, where I understand the town centre has been wiped out. On the credit side, the defences seem to have been a bit better organised and we got thirteen of the bastards. It's still nowhere near enough. Last night, just for a change, they left the ports alone – apart from Hull – and attacked Sheffield and Nottingham. They lost seven, four to Defiants."

The Boulton Paul Defiant, its sole armament four .303 machine-guns in a power-operated turret, had been a disaster as a day fighter, but was performing well against the night raiders. In just over a week of operations the Defiants had shot down fifteen enemy bombers, two more than the Beaufighters.

"Your Beaufighter Flight has been carrying out regular patrols of the Biscay area, Ken?" Glendenning asked abruptly.

"Yes, sir. Ever since it returned from Northern Ireland."

"And your crews have encountered no enemy aircraft?"

Armstrong shook his head. "No, sir. They shot up a couple of minesweepers, though, and left one of them on fire."

The air commodore frowned. "I find the absence of enemy aircraft odd. Very odd indeed. Bordeaux aerodrome is stiff with them. After we received intelligence that a reinforcement of Junkers 88s had flown in we sent out a PR Spitfire to confirm it, and sure enough, our people counted twenty-six of them. That's a substantial force, and you'd think they'd be doing something with it."

There was a knock on the door, and in response to Glendenning's command a section officer of the Women's Auxiliary Air Force came in, bearing a sealed buff envelope which she handed to the air commodore. He waited until she had left before opening it. He put on a pair of half-moon glasses, extracted the envelope's contents and studied them carefully before replacing them.

"The latest report on the Pandora trials," he said. "You'll remember those?"

"I do indeed, sir," Armstrong said, "and I'm glad we didn't have to do them."

Pandora was a scheme, dreamed up by God knew who, which involved a twin-engined bomber flying directly above a German night bomber and dropping an explosive charge on it. In the end, the job of testing it had been given to 93 Squadron, which was equipped with American-built Douglas Havocs.

"Well, the concept was tried out operationally the night before last," Glendenning said. "And, as you correctly predicted, it didn't work."

Armstrong made no comment. Equally as unworkable, to his mind, was a plan to operate Havocs equipped with searchlights in conjunction with Hurricane day-fighters.

The Havoc, which was radar-equipped, was supposed to detect and illuminate the target, which would then be shot down by the accompanying fighter. At least, that was the theory. No, Armstrong told himself, the solution to the night-bomber problem was the fast, heavily-armed night-fighter, and already there were rumours of something coming along that would be better even than the Beaufighter.

In fact, it was much more than a rumour, for Armstrong had seen one of the prototypes flying during a visit to the Aeroplane and Armament Experimental Establishment at Boscombe Down. A truly beautiful aircraft, powered by two Rolls-Royce Merlins, its airframe was made of balsa wood, spruce and plywood, which meant that it would be light and fast. It was being developed as a reconnaissance aircraft, light bomber and night-fighter. It was built by de Havilland, and they were going to call it the Mosquito.

Aircraft such as these would eventually triumph over the night-bomber, but it would take time. As it was, with the exception of the handful of aircraft equipped with radar, night-fighting was a matter of chance. But there were plenty of pilots who were prepared to take that chance, taking to the night sky in their Spitfires or Hurricanes, and Armstrong had met one of them in April, during his short stay at Tangmere.

Flight Lieutenant Richard Stevens had come slanting down out of the pre-dawn sky to refuel his Hurricane after a long night patrol over the Channel. Over breakfast, Armstrong had learned a little about his fellow officer, but not much. It had been left to others to tell the story.

When Stevens joined the RAF on the outbreak of war at the age of thirty – the maximum for aircrew entry – he was already a veteran pilot, having spent some time flying the cross-Channel route with cargoes of mail and newspapers. He had amassed some 400 hours' flying time at night and in all weather conditions, and his accumulated skill was soon to be put to good use.

Stevens's career as a fighter pilot began at an age when many other pilots were finished with operational flying. His first squadron was No. 151, which he joined in October 1940 at the tail-end of the Battle of Britain, just as the Germans were beginning to switch their main attacks from daytime to night.

It was in one of these early night attacks that Stevens's family died, turning him into a dedicated killer.

No. 151 Squadron, then equipped with Hurricanes, was a day-fighter unit; its task ended when darkness fell. Night after night, as the enemy bombers droned towards London, Stevens would sit alone out on Manston airfield and watch the red glare of fires and the flicker of searchlights on the horizon, brooding and cursing the fact that the Hurricanes were not equipped for night-fighting. At last, one day in December, he could stand the frustration no longer. He asked his commanding officer for permission to fly a lone night sortie over London, and it was granted.

His early night patrols were disappointing, for several nights running, although the Manston controller assured him that the sky was filled with enemy bombers, Stevens saw nothing. Then, on the night of 15 January 1941, he knocked two raiders – a Dornier 17 and a Heinkel 111 –

from the sky, an exploit that earned him the Distinguished Flying Cross.

By this time No. 151 Squadron was beginning to re-equip with the Defiant, but Stevens stuck doggedly to his Hurricane, stalking his victims through the night sky, aided only by bursting anti-aircraft shells, searchlights and his own exceptional eyesight. Despite the loss of his family, he felt no special hatred for the crews of the bombers he was shooting down – they were airmen like himself, following orders and doing a difficult job. Sometimes, he felt a surge of pity for the young men he was killing as he poured bullets into a bomber's shattered cockpit. But he loathed Hitler and the Nazis, and the thought of what it would mean if Britain were overrun overwhelmed any other emotion except, perhaps, sudden elation as he watched his victim fall in flames.

His technique was to stalk an enemy bomber for minutes on end, finally closing in and firing at point-blank range to make sure of his kill. On one occasion, while attacking a Heinkel from only a few yards' range, the bomber suddenly exploded in a violent gush of flame. The shock-wave flung the Hurricane over on its back and it shot through a cloud of blazing wreckage. Miraculously, the fighter was undamaged, but it was covered in oil and there was blood on the wings . . .

Shortly after the award of his first DFC, Stevens developed ear trouble and was grounded for a while. He returned to action on 8 April, shooting down two Heinkels in one night. Two nights later he got another Heinkel and a Junkers 88, and a few days after that he

received a Bar to his DFC. On 19 April he destroyed yet
another Heinkel, and the previous Wednesday night, so
Armstrong had heard, he had got two more. That made
nine enemy bombers so far, and there seemed to be no
stopping this remarkable pilot, who had quietly confided
to Armstrong that if there should ever be a shortage of
bombers over Britain, he would fly his Hurricane over to
the Continent, and go looking for them over their own
airfields.

Armstrong had heartily wished that he had come across
Stevens in the summer of 1940, when he himself had
been given the task of forming a squadron for intruder
operations. But the intruder idea had been tried out and,
for the moment, abandoned as a serious venture, while
Armstrong had moved on to other things.

"Anyway," Air Commodore Glendenning said, breaking
into Armstrong's brief reverie, "our job is to try to make
some sense out of what is going on, and be ready for any
eventuality. I think—"

He looked up in some annoyance as the WAAF section
officer knocked and came into the room again.

"Sorry to interrupt you, sir, but I think you should
see this. It's a compilation of various Coastal Command
reconnaissance reports, brought back by aircraft during
the past forty-eight hours, and some of it is substantiated
by 'Y' Service intercepts." She handed Glendenning a
red folder.

"Thank you, Sheila. Could you organise some tea for
us, do you think?"

The WAAF nodded and departed. Glendenning studied

the contents of the folder, his eyes widening from time to time. At length he closed it, sat back in his chair and expelled his breath.

"I think this is it, Ken," he said. "They're on the move. Two big tankers have been sighted off the north Norwegian coast, apparently heading for the Arctic, and four more, together with what appears to be a supply ship, have been tracked leaving the French ports. The prediction is that these are making for the Central Atlantic. What's your prognosis?"

Armstrong thought for a few moments, then said, "Well, sir, my first thought was that the *Scharnhorst* might be on the point of breaking out of Brest and heading back to Germany via the Arctic, but on reflection I don't think that's it. Half a dozen tankers seems an awful lot to support just one warship. It's my belief that they are going to send out the *Bismarck* and *Prinz Eugen*, and that when these are within striking distance of the convoy routes they'll be joined by the *Scharnhorst*. We know that the *Gneisenau* is still being repaired, so she's out of the picture for the time being. And I'd like to bet that the next few days will see more U-boats putting to sea."

Glendenning nodded. "I agree with you. And when they've made their sortie they will make for Brest, or maybe Lorient, which explains the big increase of air power at Bordeaux. It's not a pretty picture, Ken. Come along – let's go and see our friends in the Admiralty, and find out if they have any inkling of what's going on."

A few minutes later, having negotiated entry to the Admiralty building past numerous armed sentries, they were conferring with a couple of senior naval officers in one of the operations rooms. Like others deep underground, the room had escaped damage when the building itself was hit during an air raid, although there were cracks in the ceiling.

Armstrong discovered that one of the naval officers, Captain Merriman, was responsible for liaising with Glendenning on joint operational procedures between the RAF and the Royal Navy; the two met on a daily basis to update one another on information gleaned from air and submarine reconnaissance, and from various other sources. Merriman's companion, Lieutenant Commander Rawdon, was a Fleet Air Arm officer, on temporary secondment to the Admiralty from Gibraltar. It turned out that he knew Dickie Baird very well, which came as no surprise to Armstrong. The Fleet Air Arm, still a relatively small organisation, was a closely-knit community.

Glendenning told the two naval officers about the reconnaissance report. Merriman looked worried.

"It's a bad time," he said. "If the *Bismarck* and the other capital ships come out now, there'll be precious little to stand in their way. There's only the cruiser *Suffolk* patrolling the Denmark Strait; *Norfolk* is off Iceland. There are more cruisers and destroyers at Scapa Flow, with the Home Fleet, but only two ships would have a fighting chance against the *Bismarck*, if everything we hear about her capabilities is correct. They are the *King George V* and the *Prince of Wales*, although the latter is just out of the builder's yard and she's not ready for action. In fact, workmen are still on board her, trying to remedy problems with two of her gun turrets. Apart from that, there's the battlecruiser *Repulse*, in the Clyde. She's about to go to the Mediterranean. Oh, yes, and the *Hood*. But she's an old lady now, and she hasn't got much armour on her upper decks. That's a big worry."

Built on the Clyde and launched in 1916, the 42,000-ton battlecruiser *Hood* had, in her heyday, been the finest – and, with a maximum speed of thirty-two knots, the fastest – warship in the world. And the whole world knew her, for in the years between the wars she had 'shown the flag' for Britain all around the globe. She was armed with eight 15-inch guns, which made her a formidable opponent. She had been laid down before the Battle of Jutland in 1916, a battle in which three British battlecruisers had been sunk by shells which, fired at long range, had plunged vertically through their lightly armoured decks. All large British warships built after Jutland had been fitted with strengthened armour, but although the *Hood*'s armour had been strengthened on her sides, no attention had been paid to her decks . . .

"What about aircraft carriers?" Armstrong asked. It was Rawdon who answered him.

"There's the *Victorious*," he said. "She's currently out on exercise, and after that she's due to sail for Malta with a load of Hurricanes, accompanied by *Repulse*. Her air squadrons are ashore in the Orkneys, undergoing intensive training. I visited them a few days ago, and I can tell you that the aircrews are very inexperienced. It's doubtful whether they would be able to find and positively identify the *Bismarck*, let alone carry out a successful torpedo attack against her."

Glendenning looked at Armstrong. "Better get your chap Baird up there as fast as you can," he ordered. "He's a ship recognition expert, isn't he? It looks as though he's going to be needed."

"Very good, sir." Armstrong made for a telephone and got through to Baird at Perranporth after some delay, warning his second-in-command to be ready for a move, but giving no further details. He would brief Baird on the situation in the morning, when he flew back to the Cornish airfield.

"We'd better lay this latest intelligence before our respective commanders-in-chief without delay," Glendenning said. "We're going to have to get organised, and we don't know how much time we've got. I'm aware that we already have an operational task group in place to deal with the possibility of a breakout by the German ships, with various people designated for various jobs, but it will take time to pull everybody in."

"We'll get on to it right away," Merriman said. "I'll have an emergency war room set up, so we won't be in anyone else's way."

After further discussions with the naval officers, Glendenning and Armstrong returned to the Air Ministry to sketch out a preliminary operational plan to be laid before Air Chief Marshal Sir Frederick Bowhill, the C-in-C RAF Coastal Command. It was Bowhill who, in conjunction with Admiral Sir John Tovey, the C-in-C Home Fleet, was responsible for joint air and sea operations against German naval forces in the Atlantic.

"I'm worried about the build-up of German bombers at

Cherbourg," Glendenning confessed to Armstrong, "so I am proposing to leave your Beaufighters where they are, at Perranporth, to be within striking distance of them. I shall try to have more Beaufighters assigned to you if need be. As for torpedo aircraft, it looks as though we shall have to rely mainly on the Navy, because Coastal Command's torpedo-bomber resources are spread pretty thinly."

The air commodore glanced at a map of the British Isles pinned to his office wall.

"The only Beaufort squadron reasonably well placed to take a smack at the warships as they come out into the North Sea is 42 Squadron, up at Leuchars in Scotland; they might, I suppose, be reinforced by 22 Squadron from North Coates, but only if there's sufficient warning. Over at St Eval there's 217 Squadron, also with Beauforts, but we'll need to keep it there as an insurance against a breakout by the Brest Squadron."

Glendenning rubbed an index finger against his short, dark moustache.

"To my mind, the whole key to this business is effective air reconnaissance, and that means daily sorties to the Baltic by PRU Spitfires. Once we know the Germans are on the move for certain, we can intensify patrols by Hudson aircraft and submarines off the Norwegian coast. We can't risk losing the warships in that area; there are any number of fjords they can hole up in, and as you know yourself it would be a difficult job to locate them."

Armstrong did know; earlier in the War, flying a PR Spitfire, part of his task had been to keep a watch on the Norwegian fjords, searching for German merchant vessels heading for their home ports from the Atlantic. That had been before the Germans overran Norway, and set up facilities to provide anchorages for their large warships.

"Assuming – just assuming – that the Germans evade the air patrols here, and are not sighted by our submarines, it will be up to the longer-range maritime patrol aircraft, the Catalinas and Sunderlands, to pick them up," Glendenning went on. "There are two Catalina squadrons we can use, 209 at Castle Archdale, in Northern Ireland, and 210 at Oban, on the west coast of Scotland. In fact, both have detached flights at Sullom Voe, in the Shetlands, from where they fly Arctic patrols. But there aren't many Catalinas, and there's an awful lot of ocean."

"What about the Sunderlands?" Armstrong wanted to know.

"Well," Glendenning answered, "there's 201 Squadron, which is also at Sullom Voe, and 204 at Reykjavik, in Iceland. Both squadrons are fully committed to anti-submarine work and convoy protection, though, so just diverting even two or three of their aircraft for recon-naissance duty would be taking a risk. It makes the case for borrowing some Halifaxes from Bomber Command, or the Liberators from Ferry Command, even stronger. That's a matter I must chase up, without delay. Whichever way you look at it, it's going to be a gamble, unless we locate the warships immediately and never lose sight of them. And that's something we can't guarantee."

Armstrong spent the night in London, flying back to Perranporth the following morning. There were no raids on the capital that night, and for once London slept undisturbed, its inhabitants blissfully unaware of the terror that was to come only twenty-four hours later.

Between dusk and dawn on the night of 10–11 May, London lay bathed in the light of a full moon. All over England the night was fine, with good visibility apart from some haze near large towns in the south and early morning fog patches in the Midlands and the North.

Saturday, 10 May, had been quiet, the Germans confining their air activity to a few fighter sweeps off the coast and some armed shipping reconnaissances. Then, at about 2230, the bombers began taking off from the airfields of *Luftflotten* 2 and 3. Their target was London and they came in wave after wave all night long, 600 of them. Their bombs fell in sixty-one London boroughs, but the main weight of the attack fell on central, eastern and south-eastern areas. Over 2,000 serious fires were started, central London and the docks area being the worst hit. The fire services were stretched to the limit, their difficulties compounded by the fact that the Thames water level was low.

Ancient and much-loved churches whose spires had graced the city's skyline for centuries – St Clement Dane's, St Mary-le-Bow, St Columba's, and many others – were nothing more than gaunt ruins by daybreak. The Houses of Parliament, Westminster Abbey, the British Museum and the Tower of London featured in a long list of public buildings that were hit. More than 1,000 people were killed and over 2,000 injured.

Anti-aircraft Command expended 4,500 shells and shot

down one raider. Fighter Command's Beaufighters, Defiants, Spitfires and Hurricanes destroyed nine more, although in the confusion of battle over the flaming city the pilots claimed to have destroyed twenty-eight.

The Germans lost one other aircraft that night. Just after ten o'clock, as the London raiders were warming up their engines, an air defence radar station on the north-east coast of England detected an unidentified aircraft approaching British air space. As it approached the coast it dived to pick up speed, crossed the Scottish border and headed almost due west at low level. Two Defiant night fighters were scrambled from Prestwick to intercept the intruder, but it was travelling so fast that they failed to catch it.

The mysterious aircraft, a Messerschmitt 110, flew over the town of Kilmarnock, twenty-five miles south of Glasgow. When it reached the sea the pilot turned south and followed the coast for a few miles before heading back inland. He then took the aircraft up to over 6,000 feet and baled out to land near the village of Eaglesham, where he was arrested. The Messerschmitt crashed nearby. It was 2309.

Later that night, Wing Commander the Duke of Hamilton, who was in charge of sector operations at Turnhouse, near Edinburgh, was awakened with the astonishing news that the German pilot was demanding to see him. In 1936 the Duke, known as 'Douglo' to his RAF colleagues, had visited the Berlin Olympics and met several *Luftwaffe* pilots. He had carefully noted their names, but had never heard of the man who was now asking to see him – a man calling himself Alfred Horn.

Mystified, Douglo went off to Maryhill Barracks, Glasgow,

where the prisoner was being held. He entered the room where the prisoner was, accompanied by an interrogating officer and a military officer of the guard. The prisoner, who Douglo had no recollection of ever having seen before – but who claimed to have met the RAF officer at the Berlin Olympics – requested a private interview, which was granted.

The Duke listened in growing disbelief as the German identified himself. He went on to say that he was on a mission of humanity; that Adolf Hitler had no wish to defeat England and desired to stop fighting. A close friend, Albrecht Haushofer, an intellectual, had already tried to contact the Duke via Lisbon with much the same message, although Douglo had never received any such communication.

The German pilot went on to say that he had tried to fly to Dungavel, the Duke of Hamilton's home, and this was the fourth time he had set out. On the three previous occasions he had been forced to turn back owing to bad weather. He had not attempted to make the journey during the time when Britain was gaining victories in North Africa, as he thought his mission might then be interpreted as weakness, but now that Germany had gained success in both North Africa and Greece, he was glad he had come. He added that Germany would win the War – he was convinced of that – possibly soon, but certainly in two or three years. Hitler wanted to prevent the unnecessary slaughter that must inevitably take place.

The mysterious German asked the Duke if the latter could get together leading members of parliament to talk things over with a view to making peace proposals. He already knew what Hitler's peace terms would be. First, he would insist on an arrangement whereby Britain and Germany would never go to war again.

There would, of course, be certain conditions. Britain, the prisoner said, must give up her traditional policy of always opposing the strongest power in Europe.

The two talked for a while longer, and then, as Hamilton was leaving the room, the prisoner delivered his parting shot. He had forgotten, he said, to emphasise that the peace proposals could only be considered on the understanding that they were negotiated with a British government other than the present one. Winston Churchill, who the prisoner claimed had been planning war with Germany since 1936, and the politicians who supported him, were not persons with whom Hitler could negotiate.

The Duke of Hamilton returned to Turnhouse the next day, scarcely able to comprehend that the incredible interview had actually taken place, and found that two fighter pilots from the squadron he had recently commanded, No. 602, had dropped in for a visit. They were Flight Lieutenants George Chater and Sandy Johnstone. Clearly flustered, Douglo took them to one side.

"Don't think me mad," he told them, "but I've just spent half the night talking to Rudolf Hess – Hitler's Deputy!"

Chapter Thirteen

21 May 1941: 1315 Hours

High above the Korsfjord, the inlet leading to the Norwegian port of Bergen, a Spitfire described a graceful arc through the clear sky, its cameras clicking. In the cramped cockpit, Flying Officer Mike Suckling threw a quick glance behind, conscious that the enemy must be aware of his presence. The sirens on Stavanger aerodrome must be going full blast. At any minute now, Messerschmitts would be appearing over the horizon.

It was time to get out of it. His task completed, Suckling turned away and headed for home. Ninety minutes later, he was munching a hasty meal of sandwiches at Wick while RAF photographic experts rushed to develop the precious film. The Station Intelligence Officer carefully examined the still-wet prints, and came to the rapid conclusion that he was looking at a battleship and a cruiser.

On board the great battleship *King George V*, at anchor off Flotta in the Orkneys, a green telephone shrilled. The instrument was connected by a special shore line to the Admiralty in London. The officer who answered the call was Admiral Sir John Tovey, Commander-in-Chief of the

British Home Fleet. The naval staff officer at the other end of the line identified himself and said, "They're out, sir. The *Bismarck* and the *Prinz Eugen*. A photo-recce Spitfire has picked them up in an anchorage near Bergen."

The news came as no surprise to Tovey. During the night, his staff had received a signal from Captain Henry Denham RN, of the British Embassy in Stockholm. Its contents were brief, but vital. 'Kattegat today, 20th May. At 1500 two large warships, escorted by three destroyers, five escort vessels, ten or twelve aircraft, passed Marstrand course north-west. 2058/20.'

There had been other indications, too. Intelligence had already established that the two warships had completed their working-up period, and an agent in Germany had reported that new charts had just been delivered to the *Bismarck*. And there had been a very important signal from agents in France, transmitted to the special Hudson flying its nightly sorties over the Channel. It stated that the Germans were preparing moorings for large vessels at Brest. There had been an increase in enemy air activity, too; reconnaissance flights over Scapa Flow had been stepped up, and *Kondors* had been sighted over the Denmark Straits and between Greenland and Jan Mayen Island.

So Admiral Tovey knew that the warships had sailed; he also knew the route they were going to take, and their eventual destination. Thanks to wireless intelligence, he even knew the code name of the German operation: *Rheinubung*, or Rhine Exercise. He also knew that the *Bismarck* was commanded by *Kapitan* Ernst Lindemann, the *Prinz Eugen* by *Kapitan* Helmuth Brinkmann, and that the Fleet Commander was his old adversary, *Admiral Gunther Lutjens*.

What he had not known, until now, was where the ships were. And with that knowledge came the realisation that Lutjens had made two critical mistakes. The first was to pass through the narrow waters of the Kattegat in broad daylight, in full view of British agents in Sweden; the second was to enter the Norwegian fjord in order to top up *Prinz Eugen's* tanks, instead of making for the Arctic refuelling rendezvous with all speed.

While Tovey was assessing all the information, and laying his plans to intercept the warships, Suckling was in his Spitfire once more, this time in a dash to get the prints to the Air Ministry in London. A quick stop to refuel at Turnhouse and then he was on his way again, racing to beat the approaching darkness. Over the Midlands he ran into thick cloud and had to make an emergency landing at a convenient airfield near his home town of Nottingham. Rousing a friend, a local garage proprietor, he completed his journey in the latter's car, driving though the blackout at fifty miles per hour.

At one o'clock in the morning, Suckling – unshaven and still wearing his flying kit – handed over the precious package of photos to Air Marshal Sir Frederick Bowhill, Air Officer Commanding RAF Coastal Command. Bowhill studied the prints carefully – and then reached for the telephone.

Less than two hours after Suckling had walked into Bowhill's office, a force of Whitley and Hudson bombers of Coastal Command was on its way to strike at the

Bismarck and her companion. But the weather was on the Germans' side: thick cloud had descended on the fjord. Only a couple of bombers were able to locate the fjord and drop their bombs, but no hits were registered, and for one good reason: the ships had already sailed and were even now zig-zagging up the long Norwegian coastline, their anti-aircraft crews closed up for action stations. All that day the Coastal Command crews made sortie after sortie into the murk, but it was hopeless – the crews could see absolutely nothing.

At 1630 the following afternoon, with no break in the weather, a Martin Maryland reconnaissance aircraft of No. 771 Naval Air Squadron, an aircraft normally used for target-towing duties, took off from Hatston in the Orkneys and set course for Bergen. As it approached Norway at an altitude of only 200 feet, the pilot – Lieutenant Noel Goddard RNVR – peered anxiously through the rivulets of rain that streamed down the windscreen: too many Fleet Air Arm and Coastal Command aircraft had smashed themselves to oblivion on the dark crags of the Norwegian coast.

Flying in the narrow 300-foot corridor between the grey murk and the sea, Goddard sped through the entrance to Korsfjord. The thunder of the Maryland's engines echoed and re-echoed from the grim walls on either side as the pilot kept down low, allowing his observer, Commander Geoffrey Rotherham – second-in-command at Hatson and a navigator of long experience – to get a good look at the few vessels anchored in the fjord. When he pulled up into the cloud, pursued by some accurate flak that caused slight damage to their aircraft, Goddard was no longer in any doubt – the *Bismarck* and her consort had gone.

It was the news for which Admiral Tovey had been waiting, and he immediately mustered every available warship to hunt down the German warships and destroy them. Leaving Scapa Flow, the main body of the Home Fleet sailed for Icelandic waters to reinforce the heavy cruisers *Norfolk* and *Suffolk* that were now patrolling the Denmark Strait. Three more cruisers were patrolling Lutjens's alternative breakout route, between Iceland and the Faeroes.

First to arrive were the Home Fleet's two fastest ships, the battleship *Prince of Wales* and the battlecruiser *Hood*. Behind them came the *King George V*, four cruisers, nine destroyers, and the new aircraft carrier *Victorious*, which had sailed into Scapa Flow from her exercises a day earlier. The *Victorious* was not yet fully worked up; her complement of aircraft consisted of only nine Swordfish and six Fulmars, flown in from Hatston.

With her went Lieutenant Commander Dickie Baird, eager and happy at the prospect of action, and pleased to find that the commander of the Swordfish squadron, Lieutenant Commander Eugene Esmonde, was an old friend. Like Baird, Esmonde was a devout Catholic, but there the resemblance ended. The Esmondes came from Drominagh, set high on the wooded slopes of Lough Derg in Tipperary, and they were proud Irish nationalists to their fingertips. One of Eugene's ancestors, John Esmonde, had been hanged by the British during the rebellion of 1798, a fact that had not prevented his son from joining the

Royal Navy and working his way up to become captain of the frigate *Lion*. Another member of the family, Colonel Thomas Esmonde, had won the Victoria Cross in the Crimea; yet another had died in battle at Ypres. Every one of Eugene's five brothers had joined the British forces when war broke out; even his sister was in the WAAF.

The sudden switch from her forthcoming task in the Mediterranean to active duty in northern waters had caused some surprise among *Victorious*'s complement. Instead of their tropical 'whites' they were now muffled in cold-weather clothing. Many believed that their forthcoming task would be a lot less dangerous than the Malta run, although the carrier was to have flown off her Hurricanes at a respectable distance from the beleaguered island.

From the eastern Mediterranean, the news was grim. On 20 May, in the wake of a massive air bombardment, German airborne forces had landed on Crete, and the next morning the *Luftwaffe* had launched a series of heavy air attacks on British warships in the area, sinking the destroyer *Juno* and damaging the cruiser *Ajax*. The latter had got her revenge during the night, when, together with two more cruisers and four destroyers, she had intercepted a convoy of twenty motor sailing vessels laden with German reinforcements and scattered it, but by nightfall on 22 May the British naval forces off Crete were coming under almost constant air attack. Since then, there had been no further news.

There was no further news, either, of the whereabouts of the *Bismarck* and *Prinz Eugen*. It was now two days since Suckling had sighted them in the Bergen fjords. The strain of keeping a constant lookout was beginning to tell, particularly on the crews of the two cruisers keeping watch on the Denmark Straits.

At 1915 on 23 May, a young lookout called Able Seaman Newall on HMS *Suffolk*, his eyes watering in the cold, was sweeping the sea with his powerful binoculars. The ship was patrolling the ice shelf between Iceland and Greenland, and although the visibility towards Greenland was good, there was thick mist in the direction of Iceland.

It was from that direction, now, that a great black shape emerged from a patch of mist. Newall focused his glasses on it, and let out a yell loud enough to wake the dead.

"Ship bearing Green One Four Oh! *Two* ships bearing Green One Four Oh," he added, as a second sinister silhouette swam into view.

The cruiser sprang into action. As her crew scrambled frantically to action stations, her captain, Robert Ellis, ordered hard-a-port and full speed ahead, making for the safety of a fog bank as the battleship bore down on him less than seven miles away. He waited for the *Bismarck*'s first shattering salvo. It never came.

The *Suffolk* ran through the fog, her radar keeping track of the enemy ships as they passed her. Ellis held his course for thirteen miles and then swung out of the fog, taking up station in the wake of *Prinz Eugen*. By now *Norfolk* was already coming up fast, having picked up her sister ship's signals, and she emerged from the fog to find *Bismarck* only six miles ahead, coming straight at her. The cruiser's captain, Alfred Phillips, at once ordered a turn to starboard, and at that moment the battleship opened fire.

171

A few moments later *Norfolk* was surrounded by great geysers of water. Shell splinters whined through the air; some ricocheted off the cruiser's decks, but caused no damage or casualties. The cruiser reached the sanctuary of the fog bank and Phillips took similar action to his counterpart, keeping his ship concealed until she was a safe distance away before re-emerging to trail *Suffolk*.

Joint Operations HQ, Admiralty – 23 May 1941: 2200 Hours

"Well, at least we know where they are," Captain Merriman said. "The question now is, how quickly we can bring the big guns into action."

Air Commodore Glendenning looked at the plotting board, on which Wren plotters had placed counters representing the warships. "Which is which?" he asked. "Ours, I mean." The naval officer pointed out the dispositions of the various British ships.

"That's Admiral Tovey's force, with the *KG V*," he said, "about six hundred miles to the south-east. This plot here, about eight hundred miles to the south, is the battleship *Rodney*; she sailed for the Clyde yesterday for a refit in Boston, but we can use her if we have to. *Hood* and *Prince of Wales*, just here at a range of three hundred miles, are the closest: they should come up with the enemy tomorrow morning."

Glendenning, who had just hurried over to the Admiralty upon receiving the news that the German warships had been sighted, pointed to another plot, a long way to the south. "What's that?"

"That's Force H from Gibralter," Merriman told him. "The carrier *Ark Royal*, the cruiser *Sheffield* and destroyers. We've ordered them out to block the approaches to Brest, just as a precaution."

Glendenning nodded. "Good. On the air side, we'll keep the long-range reconnaissance patrols from Iceland and Northern Ireland at their present high level in case your shadowing cruisers lose contact during the night. I'm also going to recommend to the AOC that we move 42 Squadron to St Eval, alongside 22. And I've told Armstrong at Perranporth to hold his Beaufighters in readiness. Incidentally, I've managed to secure the loan of a couple of Halifaxes from Bomber Command to augment the reconnaissance force. I'm assigning them to Armstrong, and they'll be with him tomorrow."

"Well, then, it seems we've done all we can for the moment," Merriman said. "We'll have to wait and see what the morning brings."

It was a long night, and throughout it the pursuit continued through patches of fog and squalls of snow. *Prinz Eugen* was now in the lead, having overtaken *Bismarck* when the latter's electronic steering gear temporarily jammed, causing her to heel over to starboard. The shadowing cruisers were between ten and fourteen miles astern, all four warships racing on at thirty knots, the cruisers juddering and vibrating as they ploughed on through a peppermint-green sea.

Just before midnight, *Bismarck* disappeared into a snowstorm and the cruisers lost contact with her, both visually and by radar. After a couple of anxious hours *Suffolk* regained radar contact at 0250, and thirty minutes later, in improving visibility, she sighted the battleship. The cruiser's visual lookouts were having trouble with mirages, which were producing some extraordinary effects. Once, it seemed that the *Bismarck* had turned round and was heading directly towards them.

The four ships were now running south-west through the Denmark Strait, having passed the north-west tip of Iceland, and were steaming parallel with the limit of the pack ice. And all the while, the *Hood* and *Prince of Wales* were drawing closer to a fatal rendezvous.

In the cruisers, excitement mounted. Their crews had been unaware that British heavy warships were racing into action until 0445, when they intercepted a signal from an accompanying destroyer. Thirty minutes later, *Norfolk*'s lookouts sighted two smudges of smoke on the port bow, and a few minutes later they made out the shapes of the *Hood* and *Prince of Wales*. The German warships were also in sight, sixteen miles off the port bow. The men on the cruisers were about to have a grandstand view of the coming battle. Little did they realise what they were about to witness.

The signal that the big warships had the enemy in sight brought the Joint Operations Room wide awake. While the Wrens manoeuvred their counters into fresh positions, a signals officer passed on constant updates to Glendenning, Merriman and their respective staffs.

At 0553, the opposing forces opened fire almost simultaneously. Great orange flashes and huge clouds of black smoke belched from the forward turrets of the *Hood* as she fired her first salvo. It fell just astern of the *Bismarck*, sending fountains of water 200 feet into the air. The German battleship's salvo was still coming in.

0610. In the Joint Operations Room, the signals officer rose from his station and turned to face the men and women at the plotting table. His face was white with shock, and when he spoke his voice was barely above a whisper.

"They've sunk the *Hood*," he said dully.

"What?" Merriman's voice broke the sudden silence.

"The *Hood*'s been sunk, sir. That's all it says."

"Oh, my God!" At the plotting table, one of the Wrens began to weep silently.

For the ship that had been the Royal Navy's pride, the end had come swiftly. Two shell splashes rose beside her, and almost immediately the horrified spectators on the *Prince of Wales* saw a vast eruption of flame leap upwards from between her masts, accompanied by a great incandescent fireball.

The volcanic burst of fire lasted only a second or two, and when it disappeared the space that had been occupied by the *Hood* was obscured by a great column of smoke. Through it, the bows and stern of the ship could just be seen, each rising steeply up as the central part of the ship collapsed. Within a minute or so she was gone, taking with her all but three of her complement of 1,416 officers and men, including the force commander, Vice Admiral Lancelot Holland.

Captain Merriman's quiet but authoritative voice cut through the stunned silence in the Operations Room.

"All right, there's work to be done. Let's get on with it."

At 0620, the signals officer received another message.

"The *Prince of Wales* is breaking off action under cover of smoke. She's been heavily hit and has many casualties."

The destruction of the *Hood* had left Admiral Lutjens free to concentrate his warships' fire on the British battleship, and in ten minutes she was hit by four 15-inch and three 8-inch shells. One 15-inch missile wrecked her bridge, killing or wounding everyone except Captain John Leach and his Chief Yeoman of Signals. Apart from the human carnage it caused, the shells severed communications to the steering wheel and destroyed some of the gunnery control telephone leads.

Another 15-inch shell hit the superstructure supporting the gun directors that controlled the forward secondary armament of 5.5-inch guns and put them out of action. A third hit smashed the wings of the ship's spotter aircraft, which was on the point of being catapulted off; the crew scrambled clear and the dangerous, fuel-laden wreck was tipped over the side. Yet another heavy shell had penetrated the side deep under water, passing through several bulkheads and coming to rest without exploding near the diesel dynamo room. It was only discovered after the battleship returned to harbour.

Two of the 8-inch shells had pierced the ship's side aft, on the waterline, allowing 500 tons of water to pour into the ship. The third entered one of the 5.25-inch shell handling rooms, bounced around the confined space like a streak of lightning, then fell to the floor, also without exploding. By some miracle, no one was hurt.

With five of his 14-inch guns out of action, and the range down to 14,500 yards, Captain Leach had no choice but to break off the engagement. Lutjens, at that moment, might well have decided to close in and finish off the *Prince of Wales*, but he had no notion of the damage his battleship had inflicted on her.

Besides, he had problems of his own. The exchange of gunfire had not been entirely one-sided. The *Prince of Wales* had fired eighteen salvoes, and one of them had found its mark. *Bismarck* had been hit by three shells, one of which caused an oil leakage from two fuel tanks, and the contamination of others by sea water. At 0800, the German admiral decided to abandon his sortie into the Atlantic and head for St Nazaire, the only port on the Atlantic coast with a dry dock big enough to take his flagship. He would detach *Prinz Eugen* en route, to make her way to Brest alone.

Still shadowed by the cruisers, the *Bismarck* ploughed on through the ocean, leaving a tell-tale slick of oil behind her.

A Hudson aircraft from Iceland had observed the brief battle. It now circled the spot where the *Hood* had gone down, directing destroyers to the scene. The rescuers found three Carley rafts close together, each with an exhausted, shell-shocked man clinging to it. They were Midshipman Dundas, Able Seaman Tilburn, and Signalman Briggs.

The destroyers searched for a long time, the rescuers wondering what had happened to the rest of *Hood*'s crew. It was only slowly that the realisation dawned on them – there were only three survivors. The rest of her crew lay a thousand fathoms down, amid the wreckage of their ship.

Chapter Fourteen

HMS Victorious – 24 May 1941: 2200 Hours

A formidable array of warships was now converging on the *Bismarck*. As well as Admiral Somerville's Force H, coming up from Gibraltar to cut off the German commander's escape route to the south, and Admiral Tovey's force, the battleships *Rodney* and *Ramillies* were also released from escort duties to take part in the chase, while the cruisers *Edinburgh* and *Dorsetshire* were detached from escort work to join the other cruisers shadowing the enemy. The main concern now was to reduce the *Bismarck*'s speed, giving the hunters a chance to close in for the kill – and that was where the *Victorious* and her aircraft came in. At 1440 hours on the 24th, Admiral Tovey had sent her racing ahead of the main force to a position from which she could fly off her Swordfish against the *Bismarck*.

The aircrews assembled in the carrier's Air Operations Room knew nothing of the powerful reinforcements now closing in on the enemy. Baird, listening intently, was surprised when the Air Staff Officer, whose task it was to deliver the briefing, told them that the Admiralty had intercepted a signal, indicating for certain that the German battleship was heading directly for Brest, rather than St Nazaire, because of a worsening fuel situation. The signal, he told himself, would surely have been in code, and enemy codes took months to crack. He wondered how it had been done. Baird, of course, knew nothing of Ultra, or the seizure of the Enigma machine and its associated cypher books from the U-110; nor did he know that destroyer and corvette submarine killers were already making for a position in the Atlantic where six U-boats had been stationed in a line to cover the battleship's retreat, their intentions also uncovered by the wizards at Bletchley Park.

By 2200 hours the distance between the *Victorious* and the enemy battleship had closed to about 120 miles, and Captain Bovell ordered his Fulmars out to search for her, but they found nothing in the appalling weather conditions and two of the six aircraft sent out failed to return. It was a miracle that any managed to get back, and the fact that the Fulmars had been sent out in the first place was an indication of the desperation attached to the search for the enemy battleship. A two-seat fighter, developed from a lightweight version of the Fairey Battle light bomber and armed with eight machine-guns, the Fulmar was having some success against enemy bombers in the Mediterranean, but it was quite unsuited to bad weather reconnaissance work.

The briefing over, the Swordfish crews waited for the call to go into action. Baird had taken over a Swordfish in the second flight; its usual pilot was in the sick bay, having just had his appendix removed. Baird's reputation had preceded him, and his observer and gunner didn't seem to mind the change in the least.

"Hands to flying stations. Stand by to fly off aircraft."

The nine Swordfish squatted at the end of the slippery flight deck, each encumbered with an eighteen-inch torpedo slung below its belly. The deck crews started their Bristol Pegasus radial engines and the aircrews climbed aboard the big biplanes, a task made difficult by the bulk of their flying clothing.

Victorious turned to starboard, heading into the teeth of a north-westerly wind, not quite a gale but close to it, that sent clouds of sleet driving before it through the darkness. One by one, the nine biplanes bounced down the deck and into the air, climbing away laboriously. Forming up overhead, they vanished into the darkness, helped along now by the strong tail-wind. Showers of sleet lashed into the open cockpits, blinding the crews and chilling them to the bone. They flew on, maintaining strict radio silence.

An hour later, through a clear patch, Esmonde, in the lead, sighted a group of warships and identified them as the *Prince of Wales*, the *Suffolk* and the *Norfolk*. Somewhere in the semi-darkness beyond was the *Bismarck*. As each Swordfish flight passed over the *Norfolk*, a signal lamp from her bridge flashed, giving the pilots a bearing that would bring them to the enemy battleship.

The Swordfish went up into the clouds, hoping to achieve surprise as they made their attack. Baird's observer, Sub Lieutenant Nicholls, suddenly announced that he had an ASV radar contact ahead; it could only be the *Bismarck*. Esmonde and the other two crews in the leading flight had already re-emerged from the clouds and were in visual contact with the battleship, a black streak trailing a long arrowhead of wake.

The Swordfish split up and dived away to make their attacks from different directions, and almost immediately the *Bismarck* began to take evasive action. Vivid flashes illuminated her superstructure as her anti-aircraft gunners opened up, laying down a barrage in the path of the incoming torpedo-bombers.

"Here we go, chaps!" The leader of Baird's flight dropped out of the clouds to make his attack on the *Bismarck*'s port bow. Dissatisfied with his run, he suddenly turned away, then went in again, so that his aircraft and Baird's were flying almost parallel with one another.

In spite of the cold, sweat poured down Baird's body as he concentrated on holding his aircraft steady in the face of the withering barrage. He pulled a lever on the side of the cockpit, freeing a locking pin and arming the eighteen-inch torpedo. In front of him, the great black silhouette of the battleship, obscured by smoke and lit by a myriad flashes from the muzzles of its guns, was set squarely in the biplane's sighting mechanism, a bar of a dozen small lamps set on the coaming of the instrument panel.

Esmonde's flight had completed its attack and was now turning aside from the fearsome barrage. Esmonde had begun his run at a distance of four miles and had suffered damage to his Swordfish's ailerons, but he and the other two had survived.

Baird flew on through a storm of shellbursts, hearing and feeling shell splinters slapping through the fabric of his aircraft. The Swordfish, making only eighty-five miles per hour, seemed to be standing still. But its low airspeed seemed to be confusing the enemy gunners, for most of their shot appeared to be falling well ahead.

At a range of half a mile, and a height of fifty feet, Baird pressed the button on his control column and the Swordfish leapt as the heavy torpedo, with its 500-pound warhead, dropped away. It sliced into the water and ran towards the battleship, driven by its 220-horsepower motor.

Baird opened the throttle wide and stood the Swordfish on its wingtip, turning steeply away from the glowing streams of tracer that reached out to ensnare him, flattening out above the wavetops, weaving away from the deadly fire as the third flight made its attack. As each aircraft turned away, the gunners, in their rear cockpits, looked eagerly for the waterspouts that would determine whether the torpedoes had run true.

There was only one. One of the Swordfish pilots, Sub Lieutenant Lawson of the Royal Naval Volunteer Reserve, had crept around to the battleship's starboard side. His torpedo sent up a big column of water amidships, accompanied by a black burst of smoke from the *Bismarck*'s funnel, but it had struck one of her most heavily armoured points and she sailed on, her speed almost unchecked. The explosion killed one her crew members and injured three more.

Incredibly, not one of the Swordfish had been shot down, or even badly damaged, but they still had to get back to the carrier. The night was pitch black by the time they reached the spot where *Victorious* should have been, and to add to their problems the carrier's homing beacon was not working.

After a while, Baird's instinct told him that they must have flown past the carrier, and he voiced his fears to Nicholls.

"I think you're right, skipper," the observer said. "Do me a wide sweep to port, will you?"

Baird did as he was asked, and five minutes later the observer announced that he had picked up the distinctive electronic signature of *Victorious* on his ASV. The relief in his voice was palpable as he gave the pilot a heading to steer. The relief was shared by Baird, who was aware that the fuel state was fast becoming critical.

It was now raining heavily. Suddenly, through the downpour, Baird spotted a flash of light. It disappeared, then was repeated a few seconds later. The flashes came at regular intervals, and the pilot realised that he was looking at a signal projector, being swept through the points of the compass by someone on a ship's bridge. It could only be *Victorious*, and in view of the fact that prowling U-boats might be in the vicinity, someone was taking an incredible risk in exposing the light in order to guide the torpedo-bombers home.

Within minutes, wet and weary, he and his crew were stepping down onto the carrier's slippery deck. One by one, the other crews also sighted the friendly light and made their way back, until all were safely down. One gunner had to be virtually lifted from the cockpit, almost frozen stiff; the fuselage floor had been shot away from under him and he had been exposed to the elements during the long flight back. Considering that most of the crews had never made a deck landing at night before, the fact that they all managed to get down in one piece was little short of incredible.

The crews were dejected, believing that their mission had failed. But they had no means of knowing that their attack had produced an unexpected result.

The *Bismarck*'s twisting and weaving as she took evasive action against the torpedoes had aggravated the damage caused earlier to the forward oil tanks and to number two boiler room, which was now completely flooded and had to be abandoned. With water pouring in again, the ship was down by the bows, and her captain reduced speed to sixteen knots so that divers could go down to reset the collision mats and bring in extra pumps. It was more than an hour before she was able to increase speed to twenty knots, her most economical. Anything beyond that, and she would run out of fuel before she reached Brest.

Admiral Lutjens made a careful assessment of his position, seeking a way out of the dilemma. He had only a few hours' grace; the ship was now passing latitude fifty-seven degrees north – roughly the latitude of Aberdeen, in northern Scotland – and sunrise would be about 0400. With a carrier in the vicinity, a second air strike was bound to come in at first light.

He had one loophole. The battleship's radar and hydrophonic equipment told him that there were no British warships to starboard, that his shadowers were all on the port side. He knew that they were zig-zagging, a standard tactic when U-boats were believed to be in the area. At times, they were within twelve miles of his ship; at others, much further away.

Lutjens decided to take a gamble. At 0300 he ordered a turn to starboard, a broad turn that took three hours to complete, taking *Bismarck* across the wakes of her pursuers. He then ordered *Kapitan* Lindemann to adopt a heading of one-three-zero degrees. She was now steaming south-east, making directly for the sanctuary of Brest.

Joint Operations HQ, Admiralty – 25 May 1941:
0515 Hours

"Suffolk has just reported loss of contact, sir!"

"Damn!" Captain Merriman, not given to oaths, was prompted to release one at the Signals Officer's words. "How did they manage that?"

Earlier reports from *Suffolk*, based on the observations of her radar operators, still led Merriman and the others in the Operations Room to believe that *Bismarck* and *Prinz Eugen* were still in company. In fact, the heavy cruiser had slipped away as planned on the previous day under cover of a brief exchange of fire between *Bismarck* and her pursuers and was now heading due south towards mid-Atlantic.

Merriman and Glendenning turned to study the plot, with the warships' last known positions on it.

"D'you think they've parted company?" the air commodore asked suddenly. The naval officer had already been furiously considering the various options open to the Germans.

"Let's take a look at the possibilities," he said. "I reckon they're still making for France, but it's not a certainty. The trouble is, we don't know how badly the *Bismarck* is damaged. If it's only slight, she might be withdrawing to the coast of Greenland to repair it and take on oil from a tanker before going on to attack the convoys; if it's worse than that, she might even now be heading back to Germany. But whichever way the coin flips, I've a feeling that air reconnaissance is our only hope of finding her. The best we can do is cover all the likely routes, and pray."

Admiral Tovey, as they learned later that morning, was of a similar opinion. At 0730 he ordered Captain Bovell to fly off seven reconnaissance Swordfish to search the area to the north and west. Six returned, having found nothing; the seventh was never seen again.

At 0900, encouraging news reached the Operations Room. *Bismarck* had been transmitting lengthy messages to Germany, and the bearings of her radio signals had been picked up by direction-finding stations in Britain. The details were quickly passed to the operations staff, the bearings plotted on a chart and radioed to Admiral Tovey. All that was needed now was a cross-bearing to pinpoint the enemy battleship's position, and that could be provided by one of two D/F-equipped destroyers under Tovey's command.

What the Admiralty did not know was that one of the D/F destroyers was back in Scapa with boiler trouble, and that the other's equipment was unserviceable. Signals staff on the *King George V*, Tovey's flagship, plotted the bearings and got them wrong, so that Tovey was given the false impression that the *Bismarck* was north of her last reported position, instead of south-east of it.

That could mean only one thing: she was heading back to Germany by way of the Iceland-Faeroes gap.

Merriman and Glendenning, both dog-tired, stared incredulously at the plot as signals continued to come in.

"What the devil are they doing?" Merriman said. "They're turning north-east. All of them."

Glendenning saw that he was right. The *King George V*, *Prince of Wales*, *Victorious* and their cruiser screen, together with *Suffolk*, had reversed course and were heading in the wrong direction. Rear Admiral Frederick Wake-Walker in *Norfolk*, a long way to the south, continued to steer as though *Bismarck* was still making for France, as did the battleships *Rodney* and *Ramillies* and the cruiser *Edinburgh*. It was 1050.

HQ RAF Coastal Command, Northwood, Middlesex:
1300 Hours

The summons by Air Marshal Sir Frederick Bowhill had not been unexpected, and Glendenning had arrived at Northwood, occupying the high ground of north-west Middlesex on the borders of Hertfordshire, within an hour of receiving it. This was the nerve centre from which Coastal Command, in close cooperation with the Royal Navy, prosecuted its day-to-day war against the enemy. Bowhill came straight to the point.

"I don't believe *Bismarck* is heading back to Germany," he told the weary Glendenning. "I think she's still making for Brest. In my opinion, she'll steer down into the southern part of the Bay of Biscay and then turn north-east or north towards her harbour."

Bowhill was a former sailor, and knew what he was talking about.

"If I were the *Bismarck*'s captain, I wouldn't dream of making landfall on the Brest Peninsula, especially after a long detour out into the Atlantic. It's a vile coast at the best of times, with some very treacherous tides. No, any sensible chap would make his first landfall at Finisterre. The coast is less rocky there, and being in neutral Spain, the Finisterre light is still burning. He can then cut directly across the Bay of Biscay, with air cover all the way."

The air marshal pushed a sheaf of papers towards Glendenning. "Now then," he went on, "my navigation specialists have been working out some proposals for air searches. As you'll see from those copies, the idea is to send out three Catalinas on a parallel-track search, flying from fifty-eight degrees north on a track of two-four-oh to twenty-eight degrees forty minutes west, then one-eighty degrees for forty miles, then one-one-eight degrees to datum line zero-two-eight degrees from fifty degrees north, twenty degrees west. The Admiralty chaps are generally happy with this, although they want the search to be flown in reverse order, the first leg to be shortened by a hundred and twenty miles, the last leg to be extended by a hundred and eighty miles, and the patrol to be extended to twenty-nine degrees west. What do you think?"

Glendenning pondered, studying the diagrams before him. The Catalinas would, in effect, be patrolling a big wedge of ocean from west of the Bay of Biscay, out almost to mid-Atlantic, then swinging in towards the Western Isles of Scotland. At length, he said, "It looks a good plan, sir, but

I'd like to see more aircraft involved. If the weather out over the Atlantic stays the way it is, an aircraft could fly within five miles of the *Bismarck* and fail to see her. We've got two Halifaxes standing by under Wing Commander Armstrong's command at Perranporth – they're actually at Portreath, just down the road, because Perranporth is a bit on the small side – and we can use them to augment the recce force. They've got Bomber Command crews, but they are the best in the business."

"Let's do that, then." Bowhill looked at the clock on the wall. "The first two Catalinas are due off at 1400 and the third about half an hour later. Can you get the Halifaxes away by 1600?"

"I'll have to have a word with Armstrong, sir, but it should be possible. They arrived this morning, so refuelling should be completed by now."

Bowhill nodded. "Good. I should think – oh, excuse me a moment."

The telephone interrupted him. He lifted the receiver, listened intently, replaced it and then sat back in his chair, a small smile of satisfaction on his face. Glendenning looked at him expectantly.

"The Germans have been transmitting again," the air marshal said. "We've got a position fix. The *Bismarck* is within a fifty-mile radius of fifty-five degrees fifteen minutes north, thirty-two degrees west."

Bowhill rose and went over to the wall map. His finger tapped a spot in the North Atlantic.

"That puts her here, nine hundred miles west of Ireland and seven hundred miles south-east of Greenland.

She's not going home, Glendenning – she's going to France. Somebody had better tell Admiral Tovey," he added. "There are going to be some red faces in the Home Fleet."

Chapter Fifteen

"For God's sake, Stan, will you stop ringing me up?"
Armstrong said irritably. "I'll let you know if and when
things start to happen." There was an apologetic grunt at
the other end of the line, followed by a click.

It was six o'clock in the morning of Monday, 26 May,
and barely an hour since Armstrong had returned with the
second of the search Halifaxes after a seven-hour flight. The
aircraft's take-off had been delayed for some hours because
of trouble with the starboard outer engine, and when it had
eventually got away the sortie had been fruitless, as had the
first aircraft's. The pilot and crew had taken themselves off
to bed, leaving Armstrong to ponder moodily on the day's
events over a mug of coffee.

Armstrong was at Portreath, having decided to stay there
while the Halifaxes flew their search missions. Perranporth
was only about ten miles away, so he could be back at base
within minutes, if need be. The airfield, which had opened
in April, was occupied by the Spitfires of 152 Squadron and
by a squadron of Blenheims, which had arrived to take part
in anti-shipping operations. Armstrong didn't envy them;
he had experienced work of that kind some months earlier,

and the flak on German coastal convoys had grown a lot stiffer since then.

Although he had direct links with both the Admiralty and HQ Coastal Command via the Operations Room at Portreath, Armstrong felt himself out on a limb. That, he told himself, was because nothing at all seemed to be happening; a whole day had passed, and there was still no sign of the elusive battleship, even though the net around her was being pulled tighter. Admiral Tovey's warships were now heading south-east, while Admiral Somerville's Force H from Gibraltar was coming up fast with the intention of blocking *Bismarck*'s entry into the Bay of Biscay, where she would be relatively safe from attack.

The Halifaxes would be going out again later that day, sometime in the afternoon, and once again Armstrong fully intended to go with them. He decided to get some sleep, the sensible thing to do. But first of all, he took the precaution of ringing the switchboard.

"If a Flight Lieutenant Kalinski from Perranporth tries to get in touch with me," he said, "tell him to go to blazes. But say it humorously."

Just as Armstrong was wearily stripping off his clothes, and looking forward to at least six hours' sleep, a Catalina flying boat of No. 209 Squadron, code letter 'Z', having taken off from Lough Erne in Northern Ireland some two and a half hours earlier, was nearly halfway towards its search area. Its pilot was Flying Officer Dennis Briggs; his co-pilot was Ensign Leonard 'Tuck' Smith of the United States Navy, one of the Americans unofficially attached to RAF Coastal Command.

The Catalina droned south-westwards for three hours, its crew uncomfortably aware that the Operations Room staff at Castle Archdale had laid bets on whether or not they would find the elusive battleship on this sortie. The crew breakfasted on bacon and eggs, cooked in the flying boat's galley; lunch was a long way off, and by the time the aircraft reached the search area, another three hours into the flight, some of the men were feeling hungry again. It was 0945.

Briggs turned on to the selected heading, switched on the autopilot, and changed seats with the American, stretching his limbs gratefully. The morning was hazy and the Catalina flew on at 500 feet, keeping under the cloud base. Below, the sea was very rough, the foaming wave tops reaching up as though to pluck the aircraft from the sky.

"What's that?" Ensign Smith's sharp comment focused Briggs's attention on a spot about eight miles away. The shape was blurred, but it was undoubtedly that of a warship, and as they drew closer they saw that it was a very large warship.

"Close in, Tuck," Briggs ordered. "Let's take a closer look." He moved to the wireless table and began to draft a message for transmission by the radio operator.

Smith turned to starboard and went up into the cloud, intending to re-emerge astern of the ship. He misjudged the manoeuvre slightly, and a few minutes later, with the Catalina now at 2,000 feet, he sighted the warship through a break in the cloud. She was on the beam, and she was less than 500 yards away.

There was no longer any need to worry about the

warship's identity, for an instant later her upper works lit up as she hurled a furious barrage of AA fire at the aircraft. The Catalina rocked and lurched as anti-aircraft shells burst all around it. Shrapnel tore jagged holes in its wings and fuselage.

As the radio operator tapped out the *Bismarck*'s position, Smith jettisoned the aircraft's four depth charges to gain height, opened the throttles fully and headed as fast as he could for the cloud cover, hauling the Catalina away from the murderous flak. Below, the battleship heeled over as she began a turn to starboard, those on the bridge having seen the depth charges plummeting down and believing that they were under attack.

Briggs got his radio signal off as fast as possible, thinking that he was about to be shot down. It was 1030.

In spite of the battering his aircraft had taken, he continued to shadow the battleship. From time to time, shells blasted the air around the Catalina as the German gunners caught brief glimpses of the aircraft through rifts in the cloud.

RAF Portreath: 1115 Hours

Someone was shaking Armstrong awake. He opened his eyes groggily, saw an airman bending over him with a mug of steaming tea.

"Sir, you're wanted in Ops, right away. Thought you might like this, sir."

"Thanks." Armstrong sat up and took a sip of the

scalding, dark brown liquid, which was the RAF's effective antidote to sleep. He washed quickly, pulled on his
uniform and headed for the Operations Room, where
he found the Station Intelligence Officer awaiting him.
The IO was all smiles as he handed Armstrong a signal
form. The message on it was brief, but of unsurpassed
significance:

*One battleship bearing 240° five miles, course 150°,
my position 49°33' North, 21° 47' West. Time of origin,
1030/26.*

"My God, they've found her!" Armstrong breathed. He
looked at the wall map, where the *Bismarck*'s position
had already been plotted. The position report placed her
550 miles south-west of Ireland, 1,200 miles south-east of
Greenland, and just over 750 miles from Cape Finisterre, on
the north-west tip of Spain. Assuming she held her present
course, another few hours would bring her to within 500
miles of the Cornish Peninsula, just within the combat
radius of Kalinski's Beaufighters and within range of the
Beaufort torpedo-bombers at St Eval.

He called Perranporth on a secure line and contacted
Kalinski, telling the Pole to bring his crews to standby.
A whoop of jubilation at the other end of the line was all
the answer he needed.

Armstrong's next call was to the Admiralty, where he
spoke to Glendenning and asked the air commodore for
further instructions.

"Let the Halifax crews rest," Glendenning told him.

"With any luck, they won't be needed for the time being. *Ark Royal*'s Swordfish are in contact with the *Bismarck.*"

It was true. All night long, Vice Admiral Sir James Somerville's Force H had been forging ahead to intercept the German battleship, ploughing through waves that reached fifty feet in height. The wind speed over the *Ark Royal*'s deck was fifty miles per hour. Despite this, soon after first light, the *Ark Royal*'s captain, Loben Maund, had succeeded in flying off a dozen Swordfish to take part in the search, two of them covering the approaches to Brest.

At 1050, twenty minutes after Flying Officer Briggs despatched his vital signal – which was followed soon afterwards by another, saying that he had lost contact – the battleship was sighted by Sub Lieutenant Hartley, in Swordfish 2H, although he mistook her for the *Prinz Eugen* and reported sighting a cruiser. A few minutes later, however, Swordfish 2F arrived, and its pilot, Lieutenant Callander, correctly identified the *Bismarck.*

Somerville at once sent off two more Swordfish to relieve the first pair and to make certain. The other eight aircraft had already been recalled to the carrier to be armed with torpedoes, and Somerville needed to know what kind of ship he was dealing with, for a torpedo attack on a cruiser required a shallower depth setting.

Briggs, meanwhile, had regained contact with the battleship, and at 1330 he was relieved by another 209 Squadron Catalina; its captain was Flying Officer Goolden and he was accompanied by another American, Lieutenant Jimmy Johnson. The crew kept in touch with the battleship all afternoon, except for three occasions when they temporarily lost her, and came under frequent fire.

According to the latest plot the Bismarck was now only ninety miles away from Force H, so Admiral Somerville sent the cruiser *Sheffield* to shadow the battleship with her Type 79Y radar and, when the opportunity arose, to direct a strike by the carrier's Swordfish torpedo-bombers. Fourteen of the latter were flown off at 1450 in conditions of high winds, driving rain and rough seas, and some time later their radar revealed a target which their crews assumed was the *Bismarck*. In fact it was the *Sheffield*, whose presence in the area had not been signalled to *Ark Royal* before the strike aircraft took off. As soon as it was received, Captain Maund at once sent an urgent message off to the Swordfish in plain language: 'Look out for *Sheffield*.' It was too late.

The Swordfish came down through low cloud and attacked from different directions; several of them released their torpedoes before the mistake was recognised, but fortunately – thanks to a combination of effective evasive manoeuvring by the cruiser and faulty magnetic pistols fitted to the torpedoes – no damage was caused.

This first – and somewhat penitent – strike force returned to the carrier, which at 1910 launched a second wave of fifteen Swordfish. Their torpedoes had been refitted with contact pistols with a depth setting of twenty-two feet; these would not explode unless they hit the battleship's hull.

The aircraft, led by Lieutenant Commander Tim Coode, were directed to the target by the *Sheffield*, but in the prevailing weather conditions, coupled with fading light and heavy defensive fire, they had little chance of making a coordinated attack. Nevertheless, two torpedoes found their mark; one struck the *Bismarck*'s armoured belt and did little damage, but the other struck her extreme stern, damaging her propellers and jamming her rudders fifteen degrees to port. At 2140 Admiral Lutjens signalled Berlin: 'Ship no longer manoeuvrable. We fight to the last shell. Long live the *Führer*.'

In the Admiralty Operations Room, on board *King George V* and *Renown*, the latter Admiral Somerville's flagship, there was puzzlement as a succession of signals came in from *Sheffield* and from the Swordfish that were shadowing the *Bismarck*.

'Enemy's course 340°,' signalled the cruiser. But that meant the battleship was steering north-north-west, directly towards Tovey's force, which was inexplicable. Then a Swordfish reported *Bismarck*'s course as due north, then north-north-west again, then back to north.

At first, the pursuers, and those keeping watch on land, thought that the battleship was taking evasive action to avoid torpedoes. Then the full realisation dawned: she was out of control.

Shortly afterwards, five destroyers, led by Captain Philip Vian in the *Cossack*, arrived on the scene, having been detached from convoy duty. They made contact with the *Bismarck* and shadowed her throughout the night, transmitting regular position reports and closing in to make a series of determined torpedo attacks, but these were disrupted by heavy and accurate radar-controlled gunfire. Whether any torpedoes hit their target or not is still a mystery; the destroyer crews maintained that they saw two explosions on the *Bismarck*, but the survivors of the battleship later stated that no hits were made. Whatever the truth, the *Bismarck* was seen to reduce speed, so driving a further nail into her own coffin.

During the night, the battleships *King George V* and *Rodney* came within striking distance of their crippled enemy, but Admiral Tovey, aware of the accuracy of her radar-directed gunnery, decided to wait until daylight before engaging her; she had no means of escaping him now.

But before dawn, an urgent signal reached the Admiralty. A signals officer passed it to Air Commodore Glendenning who, after a welcome rest, was now back on duty.

"It's the latest from Ascension, sir," the officer said. Ascension was the code name for the nightly Hudson sortie over the Channel. The signal read:

Heavy activity at Bordeaux-Merignac. Bombers being armed and fuelled. Prediction is an early sortie against British warships engaged in hunt for Bismarck. Suggest implement air cover from first light.

Glendenning showed the signal to Merriman, then reached for the telephone.

Chapter Sixteen

The Beaufighters took off one by one, the blue flames from their exhaust stubs glowing against a leaden sky. There were eight of them, six painted black, the other two – reinforcements flown in from a maintenance unit the day before – in grey-green camouflage.

Armstrong, who had hurried back to Perranporth in the pre-dawn darkness, watched them go. So did a small knot of radar observers, left behind on this mission to save weight, and consequently precious fuel. Armstrong wished with all his heart that he were going with them, but this was Kalinski's 'show', and he had already picked his pilots.

The Beaufighters climbed away, their shapes becoming hazy and then vanishing altogether as they entered a layer of stratus cloud. The thunder of their powerful Hercules engines dwindled, and was quickly masked by the crackling roar of Rolls-Royce Merlins as a pair of 66 Squadron's Spitfires started up in their dispersals. A couple of minutes later the sleek fighters taxied out and took off, heading out over the Channel on their dawn patrol.

Kershaw came over and stood beside Armstrong, offering the latter a cigarette. Armstrong declined. Under the strain of the previous hours, he had abandoned his pipe and had practically chain-smoked a packet of twenty Players, with the result that his tongue tasted foul and furred.

"Here's hoping everything goes to plan," Kershaw said quietly, watching the receding Spitfires. Armstrong grunted his agreement, turning things over in his mind. The interception plan was as good as Kalinski had been able to make it, but a lot depended on luck. There was no doubt in anyone's mind that the German bombers from Bordeaux were setting out to attack the Royal Navy's warships, but Kalinski was banking on the likelihood that the Germans would be predictable and make their assault an hour or so after first light, with the sun behind them. Experience had taught him that this was their usual tactic.

With all possible parameters taken into account, such as the cruising speed of the Junkers 88s, estimated take-off time and so on, Kalinski had worked out an interception course which, he calculated, should bring his fighters into contact with the enemy in the area of forty-eight degrees north, fifteen degrees west, some two hundred miles due south of Ireland and about eighty miles from where the *Bismarck* was moving helplessly in circles.

On the crippled battleship, the news that bombers and U-boats were on the way to their rescue had come as cheering news to the crew, although some didn't believe it. Two U-boats were in fact heading for the *Bismarck*'s last reported position, but one had expended all its torpedoes and the other was damaged. In the torpedo-less U-556, *Kapitanleutnant* Herbert Wohlfarth had good reason to curse fate. Having used his last torpedoes against a relatively insignificant merchantman, he had suffered the frustration of seeing the *Ark Royal* and *Renown* pass by in the night, both within firing range . . .

Aboard the *Bismarck*, on the other hand, two young men had cause, for a fleeting time, to bless their good fortune, although they kept their feelings secret from the rest of the crew. They were the pilot and observer of the battleship's Arado reconnaissance aircraft. Just before dawn, they were summoned by Admiral Lutjens, who handed them the ship's log and a film of the engagement with the *Hood*, sealed in a watertight bag. The Arado was to be catapult-launched immediately and fly to France; the contents of the bag were to be delivered to Admiral Raeder, so that he would have an accurate record of the battleship's first – and very probably its last – ocean voyage.

The two airmen settled themselves down in the cockpit. As well as the precious bag, they now carried even more precious documents: scraps of paper, last messages to loved ones from members of the crew who had heard of their mission at the last minute. Strangely, none seemed jealous of the fact that in just a few hours' time, the two men would be drinking coffee and eating fresh bread rolls in the warmth of a French canteen.

The engine was started and warmed up, and the pilot signalled to the catapult launch officer, who pulled the lever that would send the Arado hurtling from the ship.

Nothing happened. He tried again, with the same result, and a hurried inspection revealed that the compressed air pipe that drove the catapult's mechanism had been severely damaged by a British shell splinter. It could not be repaired.

Dejectedly, their faces downcast and with the shadow of death upon them, the airmen climbed down onto the deck. Now they, too, would be going down into the mouth of hell.

One hundred and fifty miles to the south-west, Kalinski's formation of Beaufighters flew steadily on at 10,000 feet. The cloud layer below was broken, revealing patches of grey-green sea. From this altitude it looked deceptively calm, broken only by wrinkles; yet each wrinkle was a massive wave, and there would be precious little chance of survival for any aircrew unfortunate enough to go down into that watery wilderness.

Away to starboard the rising sun was a great red ball, climbing through layers of haze. It was already almost unbearably bright, and Kalinski stared into its glow between the fingers of his left hand, searching the sky on either side. He knew that he was in the right place, on the point of crossing the track of the enemy bombers – what he had no means of knowing was whether they had already gone past, or whether they were still between him and the French coast.

He decided to take a gamble. Waggling his wings to draw the attention of the other pilots, for he had no intention of breaking radio silence, he swung the formation round to the south-east, heading towards the French coast. Five minutes later, he knew that his gamble had paid off.

Scudding towards him across the cloud tops, like a

shoal of minnows fleeting over a river bed, came a line of aircraft – or rather two lines, one after the other. He counted eighteen in all, and quickly identified them as Ju 88s. There was no point in keeping radio silence now.

"Tally ho!" he yelled, his voice charged with excitement. "Enemy aircraft, dead ahead. Head-on attack, and make every shot count!"

Quite apart from the fact that the Beaufighters were not carrying a second crew member, who also had the job of changing the ammunition drums, the drums themselves having been left behind in the quest to reduce weight. Those already in place on the cannon's breeches held enough ammunition for only a few seconds of firing time, after which the pilots would have to rely on their belt-fed machine-guns, six of which were installed in the wings.

The Beaufighters fanned out into line abreast, each pilot selecting his target as the German bombers swept towards them. Kalinski picked the middle aircraft in the leading flight of nine – the aircraft, he suspected, that belonged to the formation leader – and held the control column steady with both hands, his whole body braced as the bomber's glazed nose swelled in his reflector sight. Forcing himself to keep cool, he waited until precisely the right moment, as far as his judgement would allow, before jabbing his thumb down on the firing button.

The cannon thudded and the image of the Ju 88 shivered in the sight. Kalinski had time for only a fleeting glimpse of the bomber's nose disintegrating, and then he was pushing hard on the stick, heaving the Beaufighter's nose down.

Robert Jackson

Oil spattered on his windscreen as he flashed underneath the bomber he had attacked.

Kalinski kept his aircraft in a dive until he had passed underneath the second formation. As he did so, he was aware of smoky lines of tracer drifting towards him from the bombers' ventral gun positions, but he did not feel the shock of any hits. He climbed steeply and turned, standing the Beaufighter on its wingtip as he came round in pursuit of the enemy aircraft. Not for the first time, he marvelled at the distance that aircraft in combat put between one another, especially if they were flying in opposite directions; the Junkers formation now seemed a long way off, and as the Ju 88 was a fast bomber, overhauling it took time.

There were other Beaufighters around him, and he made a quick count; all eight aircraft had come safely through the initial attack. The Junkers formation seemed smaller now, and with good reason – the German pilots had closed up to fill five gaps in their ranks. Smoke trails marked the death plunge of some of the bombers.

Kalinski came within range and picked another target, closing in fast now, opening fire at 250 yards. The bomber's rear gunner was on the ball – Kalinski felt a series of small hammer-blows as bullets punched holes in his port wing. He fired again, and orange flashes surrounded the Ju 88's cockpit area. The whole cockpit seemed to be consumed by a vivid red glow, and Kalinski guessed that his exploding shells had probably ignited flares. In a sudden flash of imagination, he visualised the nightmare inside the Junkers, the crew's blind panic as they tried to beat out the flames with their hands. An instant later the flames burst through the thin metal of the fuselage and the bomber started to go down, its framework aft of the cockpit shrouded in smoke.

Leaving the doomed aircraft to its death throes, Kalinski turned away, looking for another target. A Beaufighter zoomed past him and he saw by the code letters on its side that it was O'Day's aircraft. Off to one side and below, a Junkers that might have been O'Day's victim was spinning down, minus its tail and in flames.

The Junkers formation had become dislocated now, and some of the 88s were jettisoning their bombs and turning for home. Others, however, were sticking doggedly to their original course and Kalinski latched on to one of them, which had gone into a shallow dive to pick up speed. Ignoring the rear gunner's fire he put a burst of cannon shells into it from a few yards' range, and then the shells ran out. Hurriedly, he turned the machine-gun selector switch to fire and continued his pursuit, opening up and seeing his bullets converge on the bomber's port engine.

A thin wisp of smoke, thread-like at first, twisted back in the slipstream. It became denser as he continued to fire from dead astern, yawing the Beaufighter's nose so that he raked the Junkers from wingtip to wingtip. A tongue of bright flame streamed back from the stricken engine, and then the other motor also began to emit smoke, its propeller windmilling.

Dark shapes tumbled from the bomber and whirled back beneath the pursuing Beaufighter. Streamers of parachute silk appeared, blossoming into yellow canopies.

Like most Poles, Kalinski was not a forgiving man when

it came to the fate of Germans. He imagined the bomber crew's relief at successfully escaping from the burning aircraft, a relief that would soon turn to dread and terror as they drifted slowly down towards the cruel waves, with the dawning realisation that their chances of being picked up were infinitesimal.

Kalinski gained height again. The sky was empty. Maybe one or two of the bombers had escaped, but black smoke trails drifting on the wind and a litter of burning oil patches on the water below told him that most had not.

He called up the other Beaufighters, asking the pilots to check in, mentally ticking off names against the callsigns as they did so. To his dismay, two aircraft failed to respond. He asked if anyone knew what had happened to them.

"Blue Three bought it. I saw him collide with a bomber." The voice was O'Day's. Blue Three: that was Flight Sergeant Charlton. He'd been with the Beaufighter Flight for just under three months. The other missing pilot was one of the new boys.

"All right," Kalinski said. "Let's go home."

Forming up into two flights of three, the surviving Beaufighters set course northwards, climbing steadily as they went.

German radar on the Cherbourg Peninsula tracked the homeward-bound aircraft, and an operator passed on the information to Bordeaux, where it was received by the commander of the Ju 88 fighter squadron. He was in a towering rage. Frantic radio messages and calls for help had told of the fate of the German bombers, but he had been powerless to intervene. The original intention had been that the fighters were to escort their bomber counterparts, but these orders had been changed.

After parting company with the *Bismarck*, the *Prinz Eugen* had headed south to refuel in mid-Atlantic, but serious engine troubles had caused her captain, Brinkmann, to abandon his planned sortie against British convoys. The problem was that Brinkmann was keeping strict radio silence, so that no-one knew exactly where the cruiser was.

All that was known was that she was making for Brest, and that she would need air cover on the final leg of her approach. Her call might come at any moment, and so the Ju 88 fighter squadron was ordered to remain at readiness to answer it.

If only the squadron commander had been given authority to escort the bomber formation, as planned. If only the bombers had been able to get through to the British warships. They might have knocked out the British battleships and aircraft carriers, or at least inflicted extensive damage on them, compelling them to withdraw and so giving the *Bismarck* some chance of slipping away. If only . . .

If only. If only things had turned out differently. If only the *Bismarck* had not sustained torpedo damage. But she had, and she was crippled now, swerving erratically through the dawn with twisted propellers, still 400 miles from Brest, with the battleships *Rodney* and *King George V* coming up relentlessly for the kill. They had come within striking distance of her during the night, but Admiral Tovey, well aware of the deadly accuracy of *Bismarck*'s radar-directed gunnery, had wisely decided to wait until daylight before engaging her.

At dawn on 27 May Admiral Tovey closed in from the north-west, the two battleships approaching head-on and in line abreast, with just over half a mile between them. At 0843, with the range twelve and a half miles and *Bismarck* in sight, the battleships opened fire, their salvoes joined by the 8-inch guns of the cruiser *Norfolk*, which was now ten miles from the enemy and to the east of the main force.

The *Bismarck* returned the fire, concentrating at first on the *Rodney*, which pounded on through great fountains of water. On the German battleship's bridge, Admiral Lutjens watched the oncoming British warships through his binoculars, saw with satisfaction the accuracy of his ship's gunnery, and felt a glimmer of hope that the experience of the *Hood* might be repeated. Then he told himself that it was only a dream, that the *Bismarck* was indeed doomed, and that the best he might hope for was that her crew would acquit themselves with honour.

An officer appeared at Lutjens's elbow, clutching the waterproof bag that contained the ship's log and the film shot in the Denmark Strait. He asked Lutjens what he was to do with it.

"Might as well weight it down and throw it over the side," Lutjens remarked grimly. "No, wait!"

His eye fell on a steel locker in a corner of the bridge. It was armoured and watertight, designed to hold code books and secret documents. "Put it in there," Lutjens ordered.

Who knows, the German admiral thought wearily. Who knows? Some day, with advanced technology, a future generation might locate the wreck of the *Bismarck* deep down on the ocean floor. Some day, a salvage expedition might go down to her, and find the locker, with its contents still sealed inside, and bring them to the surface.

And then, for a time, the world would know how well and gallantly the ship had fought, and his own words would spring to life, and his name would enjoy a moment of glory . . .

Minutes later, a 14-inch shell entered the bridge like a glowing meteor and exploded there, killing everyone present and ripping a great chunk from the battleship's superstructure. The men on the pursuing warships clearly saw the flash of the explosion. Another shell wrecked the main director control, so that her gunfire became increasingly inaccurate.

By 1020 she was little more than a blazing coffin. All her guns were silent, but she still refused to strike her colours or sink, despite the fact that the British warships had fired over 700 shells at her. Only a small proportion had found their target, prompting Admiral Tovey to remark caustically to his Fleet Gunnery Officer that he would stand a better chance of hitting her if he threw his binoculars at her.

In the end the battleships, undamaged but seriously short of ammunition, were compelled to break off the action, and it was left to the cruisers *Norfolk* and *Dorsetshire* to close in and finish off the *Bismarck* with torpedoes. Finally, at 1036, she rolled over and vanished under the tortured sea, her colours still flying. With her, she took all but 119 of her crew of over 2,000; they had fought for their ship gallantly to the end.

Slowly, after picking up what suvivors they could, the British warships turned away from the patch of cold sea that was the *Bismarck*'s grave, marked only by a spreading oil slick, floating debris and a cryptic reference: forty-eight degrees ten minutes north, sixteen degrees twelve minutes west. Two Swordfish circled the scene once and then flew away to join the *Ark Royal*, cruising on the horizon.

Epilogue

"A good show, gentlemen," Air Commodore Glendenning said enthusiastically. "A thoroughly good show all round!" He looked in turn at Armstrong, Baird and Kalinski, giving the thin smile which was his version of a broad grin.

"And a good example of cooperation between the RAF and Navy," he added. "Without the Coastal Command recce flight, the *Bismarck* would never have been sighted in the Norwegian fjord. Without the Fleet Air Arm recce flight, her departure wouldn't have been discovered in time. Without the cruisers screening the Denmark Strait, we'd have probably lost her again. Without heavy ships to engage her – admittedly, at dreadful cost to the Navy – she wouldn't have altered course, and the aircraft from *Victorious* would not have been in a position to attack her. Without further efforts by Coastal Command and the Fleet Air Arm she might not have been relocated, and without the *Ark Royal*'s Swordfish attack she wouldn't have been slowed down so that our heavy units could overtake her. Yes, a tremendous effort, all round."

Kalinski gave a polite cough, causing the air commodore to look at him.

"Oh, good heavens, yes. I'm not forgetting your chaps, and what they did. Without them, the Germans might have inflicted substantial damage on our naval forces. They might even have bought enough time for *Bismarck* to be towed home. I understand that *Ark Royal* only had enough torpedoes for one more strike, and they might well have missed."

He caught Baird staring at him somewhat indignantly, and prudently decided to change tack.

"Anyway," he said, "the sinking of the *Bismarck* is the one bright spot in an otherwise gloomy situation. The last troops are being evacuated from Crete, where the Navy has done a magnificent job and taken a terrible beating. Malta is under heavy air attack, and Rommel is on the offensive in North Africa. He's got Tobruk under siege, and it looks as though the capture of that port is his main objective, so for the moment the threat of a strong German and Italian attack into Egypt seems to have been lifted. It's given us a bit of breathing space, time to form new squadrons in the theatre. We must have air superiority, and it's going to take a long time to achieve that. One of the problems is that our aircrews in North Africa are mostly inexperienced. What we urgently need is new blood, men with combat experience who can show the others the way, and begin striking at the enemy now."

He got up from behind his desk, went over to a cabinet and took out four glasses and a bottle.

"I take it you wouldn't say no to a little drink? Good.

214

Oh, by the way, have any of you chaps ever been to Africa?"

There was a gleam in Glendenning's eye which Armstrong found most disconcerting.

The Foreign Office, Downing Street, London

Two men faced one another over a highly polished oak tabletop. One was a senior diplomat, the other a man at the peak of British Intelligence. They, too, were sipping whisky.

"So he's decided to talk, then, our prisoner in the Tower," the diplomat said. The man opposite nodded.

"Yes, he's told us everything. Dates, times, forces involved, the lot."

"And are you going to tell anyone else about these revelations?" the diplomat wanted to know.

"Well, we'll have to tell the Old Man, of course. My God, can you imagine his reaction? He'll jump for joy. A powerful ally, handed to him on a plate at a time when he most needs one. I very much doubt whether he'll want to pass on the information."

The diplomat sipped his drink thoughtfully.

"Do you think they'll win?" he asked suddenly. "The Germans, I mean."

The man from Intelligence turned his crystal glass round between his long fingers.

"No," he said at length, "I don't think they will. They might achieve their initial objectives, but then they'll overstretch their supply lines and come to a stop. And winter comes early over there, you should know that. After all, you spent some years in the country."

The diplomat let out a sigh. "Yes, I did. Can't say I enjoyed it very much."

He raised his glass. "Well, I hope it all works out to our advantage. Let's drink to that."

They stretched out their arms over the table and clinked glasses. Of all the people in Britain, only three – themselves and Rudolf Hess, Hitler's deputy, now a prisoner in the Tower of London – knew that in exactly three weeks' time, on June the twenty-second, nineteen hundred and forty-one, Hitler's armoured divisions would spearhead the German invasion of Russia.

NEATH PORT TALBOT LIBRARY
AND INFORMATION SERVICES

1	5/05	25		49		73	
2		26		50		74	
3	1 99	27		51		75	
4	2/2008	28		52		76	
5		29		53		77	
6	E	30		54		78	
7		31		55		79	
8	1/06	32		56		80	
9		33		57		81	
10		34		58		82	
11		35		59		83	
12		36		60		84	
13		37		61		85	
14		38		62		86	
15		39		63		87	
16		40		64		88	
17		41		65		89	
18		42		66		90	
19		43		67		91	
20		44		68		92	
21		45		69		COMMUNITY SERVICES	
22		46		70			
23		47		71		NPT/111	
24		48		72			